FUNNY LITTLE MONKEY

FUNNY LITTLE MONKEY

Andrew Auseon

HARCOURT, INC.

ORLANDO   AUSTIN   NEW YORK
SAN DIEGO   TORONTO   LONDON

www.HarcourtBooks.com

Library of Congress Cataloging-in-Publication Data
Auseon, Andrew.
Funny little monkey/Andrew Auseon.
p.   cm.
Summary: Arty, an abnormally short fourteen-year-old boy, enlists the help of
a group of students, known at school as the "pathetic losers," to take revenge
against his abusive, tall fraternal twin brother.
[1. Brothers—Fiction.   2. Twins—Fiction.   3. Size—Fiction.
4. Family problems—Fiction.   5. High schools—Fiction.
6. Schools—Fiction.]   I. Title.
PZ7.A9194Fu   2005
[Fic]—dc22   2004019017
ISBN 0-15-205334-4

Text set in Bembo
Designed by Cathy Riggs

First edition
A   C   E   G   H   F   D   B

Printed in the United States of America

For Sarah

THAT SWEET BIG FEELING

I stand inside the bedroom closet, back cocked up tall against the closet wall. The tape measure sings the same old song:

four feet two inches tall.

Then into the bedroom, the minifridge, and I take out the small leather case, the cartridges. I keep the needles in an old mitten, one of those kinds without separate fingers but one big pocket for everybody. I rip apart a new bag of cotton balls. A box of Band-Aids lays open, bandages stacked like a deck of cards. I unscrew the lid from the bottle of rubbing alcohol and feel the stench tug at my nose hairs.

Cartridges of growth hormone click against one another as I arrange them on the desktop. I pick one up and disinfect the rubber disk on the tip with alcohol. Then I jab the tip of the needle into the cartridge. Holding the tube firmly, I pull out the plunger and watch the hormone get sucked out. It's not cloudy, or discolored, or floating with junk or anything—it's perfect. I point the syringe at the ceiling. Then I flick the end and make it quiver, mostly because people always do that in the movies. It still looks cool when I do it, as cool as the first time. Odors of metal, medicine, and alcohol rise from the balls of cotton as I swab my inner thigh.

I feel Mom watching me from the doorway. She taught me how to do this. It was six months ago, and we practiced on a warm Hot Pocket, pepperoni flavored. Six months of therapy, and for what?

"You know the drill," I say out loud. I can almost hear Mom's lips move with mine, forming the words. *"Think of something . . ."*

I push the plunger in for one click of my internal clock, one second, one fluid motion. The frigid bite of the hormone washes in and under the skin, or maybe it's just my imagination.

Think of something . . .

I think of my brother.

I think about the night before high school started. Mom was out at dinner and a movie with some guy, one of the many duds, a wannabe dad firing blanks.

"I don't know you," Kurt had said. "At school, you don't know me, either. Got it?"

"Got it," I remember saying.

"I don't want to hurt you," he said. Then he put a mouse in the microwave, to show how much he didn't want to hurt me. Needless to say, I didn't stick around for the fireworks.

I flinch, draw blood, just a trickle. I pull out the needle and press the cotton against my thigh. All that fuzz barely stops the stupid bleeding, and sometimes I just feel like bleeding. I wonder how long I could before I'd end up totally empty.

"That's a big boy," Mom says from behind me.

Yeah, sure.

AGAINST THE ROPES

THE SCHOOL NEWSLETTER OF
THE FILLMORE HIGH SCHOOL BOXING TURTLES

"A turtle only makes progress when it sticks out its neck."
—Anonymous

WEEK OF MAY 9–15

🐢 Don't forget the schoolwide "Casino Night Party" (theme as of yet undetermined) on June 3rd. Bring a date! And if you can't find a date, work the coat check!

🐢 Need a tutor? American History got you down? Did poorly on those college entrance exams? Ms. Wessin can help. E-mail her today for hourly rates and commuting and gas charges: kwessin@globenet.org.

🐢 There are still some parts left for the summer production of William Shakespeare's *The Merry Wives of Windsor.* Amaze your parents with plum roles like *the bartender's wife* and *vagrant #3*!

Lost: Green binder of personal information. Please don't read. Call Wendell at 798-0041 for reward.

WORK AT SOUTHWORTH MALL—Cash! Fun! Friends! Did we mention cash? Call 555-CASH.

NEW: Instant Messaging Club, Thursdays, 4:00 in the computer lab. Call Leslie: 579-9877.

NEW: Ghost Hunters Club, Fridays, 4:00 in the library. Call Leslie: 579-9877.

THE GREAT QUASIMODO

B eing fourteen and freakishly short has some perks, but not all that many. I conveniently stand at breast level, which is key. I don't always recognize girls' faces. But I recognize topographies, mountain ranges.

Like I recognize Leslie Dermott now, as she bobbles into the classroom, her chest moving one way and the rest of her moving off on an entirely different trajectory. Her upper body throws its own shadow from where I sit, low, underneath, gazing up at her beauty. Leslie is a freshman like me, but she must be older because she has a woman's body. She sticks out, literally.

The boob perk always tops my list. I spend much of my pointless time between homework and school and sleeping, coming up with the perks of being short.

Whenever I get depressed, I start a list. It was my old shrink's idea, to help me stay positive. It didn't work.

Ms. Wessin teaches, babbling about something or other.

I don't listen. Instead, I watch Leslie listen, and she seems to hang on every word. She sits in the front of the class by the open window. Her ponytail curls up like a hook, shellacked brown and standing out against the window shade.

I notice other things, things other people don't: how she chews pencils until tiny yellow splinters dot her lower lip. Her dark eyebrows, how they look almost red in her own private shaft of sunlight. I wonder why she sits alone at the front, alone in a classroom of would-be stalkers and probable friends. Why no one whispers to her, just like no one ever whispers to me. We miss out on all the same jokes together, and for some reason, that's comforting.

Every school has one like her—the girl with the handcrafted porcelain face and the body that forces you to readjust your sitting position to make room for renovations. She's smart as hell, too. I'm not talking just valedictorian smart; I'm talking shriveled-up-genius-in-a-wheelchair smart, like absolutely brilliant. Teachers love her. Other girls dress like her without her noticing—or if she does notice, she doesn't show it. She sits at her desk with that perfect Leslie posture, eyes focused on something none of the rest of us can see, like she's living in some other dimension. Every so often she pumps some lotion from the bottle she keeps on her desk and massages her knuckles and elbows until they goose-bump.

I watch her like a stalker idiot, like a total loser. My desk sits in the back, near the door. With my special booster seat, my red-and-white sneakers—hand-me-downs from an eight-year-old cousin—hover a foot above the floor. Our class is the runoff, the new kids, hard cases, brick heads, and thugs. I don't know any of their names, even after a year of witnessing their stupidity. That's what happens when you move someplace new and never make an effort to meet anyone. At least that's how I did it.

I named the kid on my right Stretch Pants because he's from some other country and wears these bulging black tights every day, no matter the shirt. Mustard sits in front of me, farting up an invisible cloud of lethal toxins whenever she shifts her immense weight. Once she even had the nerve to blame her mustard gas on me, but no one believed her 'cause everybody knows about Mustard. I have nothing against Stretch Pants or Mustard. Come to think of it, I've got nothing against anyone, really.

Except my brother, Kurt. I've got a lot against Kurt.

Now that I think of it, I don't really like Man Breasts, 'Fro Bro, Leechie, or Lucy Juicy, either. And that bald dude in back—I call him Kerouac—he looks like some reject from a science fiction movie about roaming tribes in a nuclear wasteland. Fingerless gloves with sharp studs. Pierced parts. I swear he's also a few years older than the rest of us, some held-back flunky with a brain the size of a cashew. He rolls a joint on his desk in the deepest row, in full view of everyone.

Ms. Wessin teaches.

It is already May, but the teachers at Millard Fillmore High School try to hide it, hoping we won't catch on. The windows in our freshman American studies classroom might as well be boarded up, the blinds are so thick. Only one window remains clear and bright, providing the cave beasts and mutants among us a rare glimpse of the outside world. Our pupils constrict and our pasty skin feels so good, it almost hurts. As for Leslie Dermott, she wears that freaking sunlight like she paid full price for it. I wonder how she ended up in this class anyway. In the crummy end of the school gene pool.

I sneak another peek. Looking at her hurts me, I swear. It feels like there's a hand clenching my heart in a fist and shoving it down into my guts.

It takes me a second to really see her, see her looking right back at me.

At me?

Ms. Wessin and my classmates—Mustard, Stretch Pants, Popsicle, and Zap—all of them melt into the floor, and Leslie kind of hangs there like a portrait on a wall, all face, connected to me by this green-eyed stare. Then something snaps, a nerve maybe, and my head jerks back to its straightforward position facing the front of the room.

Busted!

I stare straight ahead and fidget with my pencil. *Do something, hands! Act natural!* I beam my attentive thoughts to Ms. Wessin and smother her with my eagerness. *Teach me!* But she sits on her desk, her hair hanging down on either side of her head like wet laundry, her skirt coming up too high over her fillet-of-salmon thighs. I pretend to be interested.

I can still feel Leslie's stare on my cheek, an invisible hand slapping over and over, an imaginary swelling in the shape of five fingers. If only I had the stones to just talk to her. That courage must have gotten left behind with the rest of me. Somewhere in limbo sit two extra feet of height, some balls, and a dazzling wit.

I never seem to have what it takes, not with teachers, girls, or even my own family. Looking like a little kid really sucks; no question about it.

After class I walk across the trimmed front lawn and onto the sidewalk, where the school ends and the rest of the cruddy world begins. I don't get three steps before I hear the swoosh of denim, legs smooching against each other. Before a tingle of fear fully materializes in my brain, a girl emerges from a clump of bushes.

She wears faded denim overalls and a blue Dayton Flyers baseball cap. I keep walking, but she comes up behind me, her hand clamped around a chunk of rubber-banded brochures.

"Heya, you want a flyer?" she says. The closer she gets, the taller she becomes. She's the tallest girl I've ever seen. She waves one of the brochures out in front of me.

I stop. Pictures of disco balls and clowns cover the shiny paper. A gorilla holds a handful of playing cards, and a white word bubble leaks out of his teeth, "ROYAL FLUSH!" At the bottom of the brochure, a small white box holds the words THEME AS OF YET UNDETERMINED.

"Casino night party," the girl says. She starts to look a tad bit familiar. Maybe she sits near Leslie, shares her aura of hotness somewhere along its diluted edges. "*Hello,* the school fund-raiser," the girl says. "There's been posters up all over school for, like, weeks."

"Really?" I say. I hadn't noticed any.

"Take one," the girl says, and she thrusts the pile of brochures at me, like she's trying to plug a nostril.

"No thanks," I say.

"Come on, take it," she says, still thrusting. Her flat nose makes me wonder if maybe she was once in a fight or something.

"I don't want it," I say. I actually put up my hand to show her how serious I am about this, like I'm casting some sort of repellent spell.

"Take the damn thing," she says.

"Why? I'll just throw it away at the first trash can."

"I need to get rid of them, all right? I need to give them all away before I can go home." She shifts a wad of gum from one cheek to the other.

"Why?" I say.

"Community service, all right? I got busted for cheating on a test. So I'm paying my dues to society. Now take a stupid flyer. Take it."

I grab the brochure but don't even open it. Now I recognize her. Oil Change, Millard Fillmore's answer to Rosie the Riveter. Smokes cigarettes by the utility shed and fixes teachers' cars for extra credit. Oil Change and I have physiology together, the class where we get to dissect frozen cats. I watch her walk away and make a beeline for a couple of girls in matching silver miniskirts—Yvette and Yolanda. I take a last look at the ridiculous flyer she gave me and mash it into a pocket of my bag.

I can't see a single cloud in the sky, but above the roofs floats the long white feather of a jet stream, and everything behind it is a red gray color, like the cherry at the end of a cigarette. I start off again, heading southeast along Pasture Road toward my side of town. The air carries the smell of wet pavement.

I pass some of the suave developments at Pinewood Terrace, with their long brick walls out front and gold plaques on the gateposts. Southworth Mall comes up next on my right, a long strip with most of its spaces vacant, FOR LEASE signs written in marker and taped to the doors. No one ever goes to the mall, anyway, except for skateboarders who dare one another to press their bare butt cheeks up against the bagel shop windows.

A group of punks clustered around a mailbox hear me coming and start clapping. Several of them rise to their feet and give me a standing ovation.

"Yo, Shot Glass, give us a holler!" one kid shouts from behind the human shield of his buddies. His dyed hair looks the same sickly pale color as that layer of skin you get when a cut first starts to heal. A chain swings back and forth as he moves, one end connected to his ear, the other to his nose. Nose Chain and his buds have this funny midget walk they do, scrunching in their arms and making their legs all bendy to get closer to the concrete. Red pins flash on their leather jackets.

I ignore them. They don't look like midgets, anyway. They look more like that dude Igor from those old Frankenstein movies, and everyone knows that he was a hunchback. There's a big difference.

A change in scenery takes place when I arrive in my neighborhood. Once you pass the mall, Southworth's bones and guts rise to the surface. Crumbly sidewalks. Gravel driveways. Thick rusted manhole covers with dates stamped on them. Just enough abandoned stores and garbage to make strangers nervous. Houses so flimsy they'd blow over in a strong wind.

Behind me, only a couple of blocks to the north, spread field after field of cow pasture used by the community college's agricultural lab. Once, one of those stupid cows wandered off and found its way to my dumpy old street, only to get nailed by some SUV. I saw the whole thing from my front window.

My house sits in the gloom of a pair of walnut trees. They sag against the roof like they're trying to keep from fainting, and it gives the whole structure an unsteady appearance. All the dead grass makes the lawn look like the skin of a coconut. No matter how many times we spray it with fertilizer, it still stays dead.

This used to be Grampa's house. Mom moved us in here a year ago, after an ambulance trucked Grampa off to the hospital. He never came back.

I ease the front door shut to keep it from slamming.

I climb the first flight of stairs, turn the corner, and go up to the attic. This is where I live. I chose it. It was Grampa's room, and now it's my room, and it should be my room. Hunchbacks and freaks deserve tower rooms with inviting views of the bustling world below. Someday I will shake my shrunken fist at the world below and bellow, "I am Quasimodo, and I am not an animal!" Then I will slide my chains along the floor to keep the family below from sleeping.

I ease my door open, drop my backpack on the floor, and click on the green banker's lamp on my desk. Mom knows this carpenter who makes most of my midget junk for me, and this desk is my favorite. I'm not too small to use most furniture, but desks can be a real pain. Either the desk hangs too high or the seat droops too low. The desktop has a thick and sappy wood finish, a bit see-through, like that amber stuff that prehistoric bugs get trapped in. But the best part is the rolling top that covers the cubbyholes and locks with a small key I keep in the bottom drawer. It looks like some famous dead writer's desk. Picture Shakespeare as a midget. Poe as a gnome. Teeny-weeny Hemingway.

A photo of my grampa sits in a silver frame on the desktop. It's the only one I took from the moving boxes.

I examine my pathetic attic room. From school to home, one cage to another. Another week come and gone.

The moped pulls up. I hear it coming blocks away. A screech, and then the sound of heavy feet ricocheting down our vacant street. I stand up, walk across the squeaky floorboards, and shut the bedroom door. Downstairs the front door bangs—a gunshot—and I jump in my tiny red-and-white sneakers. I hate this. I hate this routine. I carefully pull the switch on my banker's lamp and sit in the dark, curling into a ball in my chair. I try to read my homework, but I can't see. I don't dare turn the light back on.

UNiCyCLE

That Sunday afternoon I lounge on the couch in the living room, the windows making boxy sunbeams on the carpet.

I can pick out each one of Mom's frizzy neck hairs in the light as she sweats and squeaks on the stationary bike. She pedals like she's filled with the Holy Spirit.

"That's right," she says, blowing by some chump with a newspaper under one arm and a blue umbrella under the other. His baseball hat flies up in the air. "Here I come," Mom says. "Who da man now?"

Mom watches a video of the streets of Paris from a driver's point of view. It is part of a video library she bought off the Net. She tells all of her friends that she's biked the world: Rome, London, Shanghai, Frankfurt, and St. Petersburg. She always fails to mention the tapes, or the leotard.

I love my mom. She looks just like some half-full pink water balloon in her leotard, jouncing and jiggling through the streets of Paris.

I like to watch her ride. It is absolutely mesmerizing to see her working so hard to go nowhere. It's also good because when she bikes she's home, which means she's not out at her killer job as assistant to the law firm of Sweats-a-Lot and Nose-Like-a-Pickle. We hardly see her anymore. By "we" I mean my twin brother and me.

I sit on the love seat by the back window of the living room, staring at Kurt and willing his head to explode. It isn't working. It never does. Two of Mom's cigarettes still smolder in the coffee table ashtray, leftovers from before the Tour de France. I squint at Kurt through a gray layer of smoke.

"Kurt, honey," Mom says when she catches her breath. "Kurt?" But her attention returns to the bike. She lurches to the side just in time to dodge a Fiat. "Mrs. Reinhart called this afternoon. You know, Grant's mom?" Her black hair sticks to her forehead in sharp downward daggers.

Kurt finally looks up from his seat at the kitchen table, where he reads a smooshed comic that's got coffee rings stamped all over the pages. "Yeah," he says. "I know who she is, Mom."

"Well, you know she *is* the nurse at your school," Mom says. "You do know that, right?"

"I'm the one who told you," he says. Getting up, he opens the fridge and tears a Coke off a six-pack.

"Well, she was telling me that one of the students had his car vandalized last week."

The bike starts beeping, and Mom lifts her legs away from the pedals. The wheel slowly stops, hissing like an old record player. She whips a towel off the arm of the couch and drapes it around her neck, an end in each hand. "The whole car was spray-painted red from top to bottom, inside and out," she says. "Can you believe that? Patty Reinhart says that whoever did it didn't miss an inch. Even the glove compartment."

Mom rocks her head back and forth like it's coming loose. "Who would possibly do something like that?" she says, raising an eyebrow and sliding the towel up and down her neck, waiting.

"Kurt's never been very artistic," I say from my cushion. "Besides, monkeys like him have trouble with simple tools like car keys and paint cans."

Kurt's big bloodshot eyes turn in my direction. "I didn't do anything," he says. "I told you I stopped screwing off, didn't I?"

"Look, Mom," I say. "It's trying to communicate. Maybe you should try sign language."

Mom snaps me a look, and I wonder if she's about to snap to the towel, too. "Arty, do not even start blowing this up into nothing. You keep yourself under control for once."

"Yeah, put a leash on it, you little turd," Kurt growls.

"Boys!" Mom says, clapping her hands together so they make a sharp cracking sound. "Enough."

Too bad. Mom used to have the ability to see through Kurt's crap. It came from having married Dad, another guy who was about as reliable as a knockoff watch. Dad went on to steal a car and rob a pharmacy. Even Mom never saw that one coming, and she's been trying to prevent a rerun with Kurt ever since. We all kind of wrote Dad off after that episode.

"Anybody could have tagged that kid's car," Kurt says, and takes a swig of his Coke. "Sucks to be him, though."

"You sure you don't know anything?" Mom says. But Kurt just drinks his pop and reads his comic, which was my comic until yesterday, when he took it out of my backpack.

"Nope," he says. "I heard about it, that's all."

I can tell by the look in her eyes that she believes him. Poor Mom, so deluded. Like Kurt hasn't done that kind of thing before. Like he didn't once pee in the gas tank of every teacher in the middle school math department. If she believes him, she'll believe anything.

Part of me wonders if she really thinks she's biking Paris, too.

Kurt yawns, cracks his knuckles, and then stretches, the floorboards groaning under his size-twelve high-tops. When not slouching, Kurt sways at six feet and one inch, no doubt enjoying better weather up there than I get down here. Life must be sunny at six feet one. Never a chance of rain.

"I'm going out," Kurt says.

"Don't forget to take Arty over to the store on your way," Mom says. She maneuvers to block the hallway door with a pink spandex shoulder.

"Can't you take him?" Kurt says.

"You know I have to go in to work today," Mom says. "You think I like it? Come on, Kurtis. Don't be a jerk."

"Fine," he says, turning away, leaving her leaning in toward the now empty space. "Arty, Arty, Arty," he bellows as he stomps down the hall.

Mom stays leaning that way for a minute before straightening back up. Kurt tramps out the front door, pausing only to punt my backpack across the entryway.

"Arty," Mom says, turning around, "get your bag. Don't make your brother wait. His fuse is short enough as it is. He's got a lot on his mind."

"Like what?" I say from across the room. Kurt never needs a reason to be a piece of crap.

"Like a girl," Mom says, and takes a bottle of water from the fridge. She slugs it back.

"What girl?"

"Someone named Mary Fielder," she says, winking. The pendant I made for her bounces around her neck. She still wears it after all these years. I got the pieces from some dump, a small silver drain from an antique sink, and I polished the shine up like crazy and tied it to a thin leather cord. She never takes the thing off.

"You sure you want to go to the store alone?" she says. I nod. "You could come to the office and help me collate briefs. I know you've been itching to alphabetize."

I climb off the couch and walk over to my mother. She bends over, flicking my right ear with a finger. Then, using her thumbs, she smooths the collar of my shirt and smiles at nothing really, kind of off into space and silly.

"What?" I say.

"Oh, nothing," she says, still smiling.

"Are you on drugs?" I say. "You can always tell me if you are. I'm not only your parent, but I'm also your friend."

Mom chuckles. She's the only mom I know of who chuckles.

She takes a step back and zips the towel off from around her neck and then cracks it at me a few times like a whip. She stops after a couple of pathetic tries and pushes me back on my heels with a towel-wrapped hand. "I was just thinking about when you two were babies," she says, her smoky brown eyes smiling right through me again. "Do you remember the tape measures that Gramma and Grampa hung from the wall when we came to visit? You know, in the front hallway where your granddad had that ugly-ass clock?"

I do remember, mostly because one of them is taped up in the back of my closet. Back in the old days, Kurt and I were always the same, dead even every time, a photo finish. "Yeah, I remember."

Mom shakes her head, then strolls back to remount her squeaky steed and ride off into the video sunset. Maybe in the world of her exercise tape, she has a handsome husband, a better job, and two normal children.

Outside, Kurt keeps an eye on me as he checks the oil on his clunky 1980-something Yamaha moped. He slides a McDonald's napkin across the dipstick to clean off the excess oil. He glares, and his blotchy face reminds me of one of those shrink-wrapped packages of ground beef you see in the grocery store. When he had his growth spurt two years ago, the acne exploded in the center of his face right around the bridge of his nose. It was like someone dropped the atomic grease bomb right on his schnoz, and the rest of the face got zit fallout.

I'd give anything for those raging hormones. I'd siphon him as if he were a gas tank.

Since then nothing's been the same between us. We don't look or feel like twins, even though we're only fraternal. We're not even the same species anymore. I'm the human one. He's something else altogether.

My heart kicks like a baby. Sweat slides down my back and into my pants, finding its way to my butt crack. Down it goes from there. Then Kurt puts that stony glare of his point-blank on my face.

He drops the blackened napkin into the gutter and grinds it into the sludge with his shoe. Then he jumps on his moped, cramming the keys in the ignition. The engine doesn't catch at first.

Scowling, he kicks the starter. It's scary how I can still see the old Kurt behind that new face, behind those puffy red welts and beady eyes. He has to be under there somewhere. Has to.

Then he speaks. "You're totally screwed if you think I'm giving you a ride to the goddamned grocery store."

The moped hacks and burps and growls to life. He guns the engine over and over. Then he peels out, snagging road, laying rubber, sputtering down the empty street with that stupid McDonald's napkin stuck to one shoe like a white flag someone wiped their muddy feet on.

I probably won't see him until tomorrow. That's how Kurt works—he'll vanish for hours doing who-knows-what in god-knows-where.

If I had my choice, he'd stay there.

As always I start hoofing it to the store. I check my watch, then curse and pick up the pace. Short legs make for long walks.

THE PENNY PARADE

All Monday long, things went according to plan, meaning I didn't get tripped, spit on, pushed, or depantsed by roaming a-holes who have nothing better to do than terrorize the small kid.

I thought I was home free, delivered from evil and all that. That is, until after last period, when I stepped outside to find him lurking by the teachers' parking lot.

Kurt was not supposed to be there. Kurt *is* not supposed to be *here.*

But he is. He smokes an unfiltered cigarette by the parking lot bushes. Balls from tennis practice pong off the fence a foot from his face. Yet he hardly notices. He focuses on inhaling and releasing, threading a thin smoky needle in the air, which is probably the most productive thing he's ever done in his entire life.

Kurt hates school. I don't think he even bothers to show up for class most of the time, and he sure as hell doesn't stick around for extracurricular activities. I can just imagine Kurt on the debate team. His rebuttal would be a fist to the other guy's brain. Like clockwork Kurt vanishes after school, and that's if he even comes in the first place.

But lately I've spotted him hanging around, always smoking, always alone, but so damn smooth. Like there's no chance in hell that a stray tennis ball might jump the fence and smash his face inside out.

I just want to go home. But he blocks the intersection at Pasture Road, my private escape chute.

I stand and wait in the shadow of Millie the Boxing Turtle. Millie is Millard Fillmore High's school mascot. She is a statue made from some kind of rough brown rock, and she towers about ten feet over the mowed front lawn. Her biceps seem to ripple, poised to deliver the old one-two punch to any rival mascot that happens to wander onto our school grounds. I hide in the dark shadows by her feet, next to the plaque that says: A TURTLE ONLY MAKES PROGRESS WHEN IT STICKS OUT ITS NECK.

When Kurt looks the other way, I dart across the exposed sidewalk and back through the front doors. I cut across the empty cafeteria, where two girls sit on a foldaway table giving each other tattoos with a needle and ink from a broken black pen. Paper banners hang from the cafeteria walls, new additions since lunch that say:

MARK YOUR CALENDARS
JUNE 3
SEND IN THE CLOWNS . . . FOR CASINO
COSTUME NIGHT—PARTY! PARTY!
(THEME AS OF YET UNDETERMINED)

Nudging the back doors of the cafeteria, I scout the area outside for potential threats.

Kid with No Legs sits by the steps in his wheelchair. Though he's not alone, he talks to himself like he is, talking trash about his parents. He says that they don't speak to him but to his disability. Their whole life is one big conversation with the legs he was supposed to have but never got. I've heard it a million times.

Kid with No Legs needs Albino Girl to spoon pudding into his mouth because his hands spasm all over the place and he can't feed himself. Albino Girl wears special goggles so she can go up and down stairs and ride a bike without falling off.

The two of them wave at me. I wave back and manage a rare smile. I know they don't want pity, because I never do, either. But I can't help feeling some for those two.

Since I can't take Pasture Road southeast, I'll have to come up with some other way home—one that Kurt doesn't know about. I sure don't want to bump into him outside Pinewood Terrace, where he can put on a macho show for the rich folks and tear me a new one. I have no choice. Not if I want to get home with all my teeth present and accounted for.

The empty underclassman parking lot steams in the heat. A dark shape shimmers, a mirage several blocks away on the sidewalk along Old Quarry Road. People. Lots of people.

If I go east in the direction of the old sandstone quarry, I can eventually cut south across the cow pastures and into my neighborhood. It might take me an extra couple of minutes, but it'll be worth it if it saves me the pain of getting my neck stepped on.

The faraway crowd already shrinks into the horizon, moving quickly across the dark profiles of trees and pointed roofs. Behind me the afternoon sun gives me a giant's shadow, legs perfectly straight like circus stilts—it must be a sign. I hoist my backpack over a shoulder and get a good grip on my booster seat. Then I take off straight east down the sidewalk. There's safety in numbers.

When I catch up, I see clearly that the kids are nothing more than a ragged caravan of ratty clothes and nappy haircuts. Like some after-school teenage death march. I recognize most of them right away. They're the army of weirdos from the school's arts wing, a basement underworld with few teachers and, from what I hear, a collective grade point average of 1.3. I see Mustard, Gravy Train, Zap, Fingers, Wiggle-It, and Battleship, all strung out along the line, and of course, there's that bald dude, Kerouac, bringing up the end, slouching along with a wilting cigarette in his fingers.

Kerouac is trouble.

After a whole year of school, I know enough to avoid him like a water fountain in Mexico. Every Saturday he grinds his skateboard on the stair railings at the public library, scattering kids and parents like pigeons. Once in a while he even starts fires in the book drop-off slot. At least that's what I heard, and I believe it. All he ever reads is this battered copy of *On the Road* that he always keeps in his back pocket.

I fall in several feet behind him and try to go unnoticed. A red-and-black tattoo pokes out where his leather jacket and camouflage pants separate—a snake's triangular head. The rest of it spirals up somewhere under Kerouac's shirt on the unseen twists of his spine. His bald head gleams in the afternoon sun, sweaty, occasionally dropping a bead onto the slick collar of his jacket.

Suddenly he notices me, and stops to turn around

very slowly. Kerouac is much taller than I remember. He looks down from a million miles away, like he's Kerouac the cosmonaut. "Arty, my man," he says. "I thought I saw you back there. How's it hanging?"

I act cool, so as not to come off like a total wiener. "I'm okay," I say. He smells like pine-scented floor cleaner, a fake chemical smell that's supposed to pass as natural.

"I've always liked that booster-seat thing you got," he says. "Pretty cool shit. You should sticker it up. I got some great ones you can have—doubles, I mean."

"Thanks," I say, kind of surprised. Who would have ever guessed that this guy collects stickers and thinks high chairs are cool or even knows my name?

"Walking with the rejects today?" he says. "You've been going to Fillmore for a whole year, bud. Why'd you wait this long to cross over? You afraid to be seen with the mole people?"

"No," I say, *yes* being the real answer. "I heard this way was faster."

"It's a nice stroll," he says. He flicks another cigarette out from a striped pack like it's a switchblade. Then he scratches a flame from a rumpled matchbook, lights the cigarette, and inhales deeply. The sun bounces off one of those pins stuck in his leather jacket collar: a red *A,* probably for *Anarchy* or something like that. "The glory of Southworth is that you can get home without ever having to go through the projects if you don't want to," he says. "You can live your whole life here and never even realize that the other half exists. But we're here. Oh yeah. And for most of us, Arty-man, the east side is home, quarry and all."

I don't tell him that my neighborhood is just a step up from the projects, like the projects-in-waiting. Give it a decade.

The kid I call Arachnid drops back a few steps to walk with us. His skin color matches the bleached ceramic of your run-of-the-mill toilet. It looks almost transparent in the bright afternoon sun. I call him Arachnid because of the Spider-Man T-shirt he wears pretty much every single day.

"What are you doing here?" he says to me. He says it in a snobby way, and it occurs to me that we've never spoken to each other before. I've never talked to any of these guys.

"Just walking," I say. "What do you think I'm doing?"

"Take a deep breath," Kerouac says, patting Arachnid on the shoulder and laughing. His eyes flick to me and widen. I can't tell if he's doing it on purpose or what, but it calms me down. "Arty's with me," Kerouac says. "He's cool. He's part of the party. Right, Arty, my man? Check it out, *Arty* rhymes with *party,* doesn't it?"

"I guess," I say. I've never been part of any party that I can remember.

As Old Quarry Road rolls on, the landscape seems to decay right in front of us, from pretty residential property to a crumbly industrial wasteland. The soil turns rocky, and the street tapers off into dust under a CAUTION sign. Fewer and fewer trash cans line the street, replaced by huge, yawning Dumpsters filled with couch halves, slabs of plywood, and piles of faded clothes. Not hesitating for a second, the caravan trudges on, into the kicked-up dust and trash.

I notice a few flat buildings way up ahead, rising over the tree line. I hear the distant moaning of cows.

"How far does this road go?" I say. It looks sort of familiar.

"It passes the quarry on the left," Kerouac says. "Then it goes on a bit more to the old abandoned Snud factory. That's where most of the projects started, as company housing for all the dumb-asses who worked their butts off for nothing. See, the east end of school is like a straight shot for us project dwellers. We're used to the dust from the old coal mines down in the quarry. Don't know how we breathe the clean stuff out in the regular world." Kerouac smiles. "This ain't the easiest walk in the world, but the view is pretty bitchin'."

The quarry. I know about the quarry. I've seen it. Once Grampa drove me down there in his beat-up truck and pointed his knobby finger all around at the grungy cliffs and steam shovels. He worked there for the last ten years until his retirement. The sandstone ran out at about the same time. Before the quarry, Grampa mined coal in shafts about an hour outside of town. The shafts and cliffs are what paid his bills, put food on his table, and eventually gave him lungs like two burned cheese omelets.

Another kid drops back from the group and falls in beside us. In his left hand he holds a ratty paperback called *Space Chix Need Lovin'*. He drinks a can of pop with the weird name *Wowzers Soda* printed across the aluminum. His red clown hair occasionally gets stuck in his mouth when he drinks. Naming him Sirloin was easy for me back in the day. He smells greasy, like a college football tailgate party.

Sirloin yanks his hair into a messy ponytail as he sidles up to me. "Yo, Moore. Is this your first penny parade?" he says to me. "A virgin?"

"My first what parade?" I say.

"It don't matter," Sirloin says. A ball of tape holds his glasses together. One of the lenses makes his left eye seem to bulge. "You picked a crapper of a day to come," he says. "Baumgardner told me the wrestlers been saving up their change since spring break."

"What for?" I say.

"You might just find out in a minute," Kerouac

says. Scraping dried gunk off the end of his nose stud, he sighs and checks his watch, a classy gold kind, though the band is black leather and sports raised metal studs. "It's been a while since they've had one. They like to stagger them out to keep us on our toes." He bends over and softly pinches my shoulder. "A few words of advice: Stay close to the ground and don't hang in one place too long."

A weepy half smile, half frown stretches across Sirloin's triangular face, and I notice that one of his teeth is a dead gray clay color. A strange coldness washes over me, and I feel very alone.

Then, growing above the murmur of the march, I hear engines. Kerouac grinds his cigarette into the bottom of his boot. The roar grows louder.

On some sort of signal, the formation breaks and kids scatter across the rubble by the side of the road. Some leap over the hoods of burned-out cars while others kiss the dirt behind the Dumpsters, their faces powdered with dust and mud. Only a few stay on the sidewalk—the older, braver kids, huge dudes with ponytails and black jeans and boots with steel toes. Kerouac sticks around, too, and he slouches almost oblivious, still working hard at that dried gunk glued to his nose piercing.

"You should hang out with us this week," he says, totally relaxed. "You'd dig it, man. We do some seriously radical shit. We're going downtown tonight, haul out the cardboard and break-dance. Carl's gonna tape it and everything. I'm telling you, you'd totally dig it."

I don't even know who Carl is, and I don't care. Break-dancing for Carl is the last thing on my mind. I want to know why fifty kids lie flat on their stomachs around me, peeking up over recycling bins. I want to know what that sound is. Cars? Tons of cars, engines, thundering like cannons.

Then they arrive, and swing around the end of the street in a single-file line of professionally washed paint and polish. Our classmates, the kids who can afford to drive home instead of walk, aim right for the rest of us. I recognize them by their makes and models. No names, just cars, wheels, and twinkling hood ornaments.

Then I hear a new noise—a hiss—and I flinch at the pain without having to think.

A cold peck on my cheek like an ice cube from a slingshot, like one of my injections but stabbed into the side of my face instead. My hands fly up to cover my eyes, and I go down with a sting tearing across my left kneecap. I'm hit again. Worse. As my shins buckle and my knees scrape sidewalk, pennies soar through the air around me.

Through the web of my fingers, I see Kerouac now wrapped in his leather jacket, the cigarette waggling ash all over his lap. Arachnid and Sirloin bend like a couple of Chinese acrobats, forming a protective barrier around him. I start to wonder why they're blocking for him, why they care, when a penny ricochets off my scalp, making the inside of my head shimmer gong style. I curl up in a ball. I can smell my armpits this close, see the caked dirt in the folds of my elbows.

The sidewalk chimes. Windows ping nearby but don't shatter. Kids scream and yelp. Others cuss at the top of their lungs, cursing God and screaming at the sky.

The cars pass until only a few bring up the rear. A voice groans from behind an uneven stone wall, a sob. A girl's voice comforts the sob, makes it a whimper. Some of the coins on the sidewalk glint weakly like the glitter we used in kindergarten craft class. So similar it's almost scary. Kurt and I used to draw pictures of each other then. On went the glue, and then came the glitter. But with Kurt and me, nothing ever worked right. The glue always ended up in my hair. So did the glitter.

I touch my head and wipe away blood.

As if drawn by the smell, Kurt brings up the rear of the parade, his moped clearing its snotty throat up and down the block. A Mercedes glides past, honking, then Kurt, and then it's over.

So this is the reason he was hanging around. He's

been joining in the penny parades. He wants to freak out all these pathetic losers, and now I am one of these pathetic losers.

A drop of blood reaches my ear, and I wipe up its long trail, all the way to the top of my head, where a lump rises. I watch Kurt ride down the street until he blends into the growing shadows. Now I have to go home and see him. It never ends. This is my life.

I get up and wipe my hands on my pants. The sun has begun to sink. The other kids drift in the dimming light like phantoms, caked in the dust of the quarry road. Arachnid and Sirloin stand together by a construction barrier and argue. Sirloin waves a finger and refers to a Dungeon Master's manual he's pulled from his backpack. It's like nothing ever happened.

Kerouac dusts off his leather jacket and ignites a bent cigarette with the last of his matches. He doesn't say a word, and together all of us start picking up the pennies.

NICKED

My head still bleeds. Still. Drops of blood soak my green shirt this muddy dog-poo color, and I could just kill my brother.

When I get home, I sit down on our front porch and take a folded-up homework assignment from my hip pocket and use it to blot my wound. Behind me our screen vibrates as voices rise and fall in the kitchen. Kurt stomps on the linoleum floor as Mom juggles silverware. Sounds like the knives. That's weird. She's hardly ever home for dinner.

A small breeze rustles the few sad blades of grass on the dead lawn and makes the plastic DO NOT STEP ON GRASS flags tremble. Grampa tried to grow grass before he went into the hospital, but nothing ever happened, and after he died we just left those little signs poking out of the ground.

"I don't know. I don't know," I hear Mom say through the screen. She fills something—dinner glasses, I guess—with water from the tap. "You've been stomping back and forth down this hallway since you got home, and all I did was ask if everything was okay. Well, is it? I can't read your mind, Kurtis."

"I don't know what to do," he says. A chair squeals on the tile. I think he kicked it.

"Sure, fine, okay," she says. "You don't know what to do. That's okay. Is that what you want me to say?"

It's weird, because Mom and Dad never fought like this when Dad was still around. Maybe it was because he was hardly ever around in the first place. The times I saw him passed quietly, peacefully, as though Mom was afraid she'd disturb the smooth surface if she said anything. Like when you have a dog sleeping next to you, and you don't move even though you want to, because you know he'll get up and move to someone else the second you twitch. Dad was like that dog, I guess.

A deep thud wobbles through the drywall. "I'm trying so hard," he says in that deep voice like a growl.

Mom's voice gets softer as she moves across the kitchen. "I'm sorry. I didn't mean to jump all over you. But sometimes—I mean, really, Kurt, the words you say are like right out of some book written by your dad. Look at me. I know it's tough."

"It is," he says. Was that a sniff? Is meathead going to cry?

"But there's one thing your father never would have said," she says.

"Yeah, what?" he grunts.

"'I'm trying so hard.'"

It's so sweet, I want to put my fist through the porch floorboards. What is this? He's "trying" what, to kill me? He could come out right now and finish me off if he wants to. Look here, I've already got blood all up and down my ugly face. See how easy it is. I've never heard them talk this way before, just Mom and Kurt without me, like they're in couples therapy or something. It pisses me off, and I'm already pissed off enough right now.

Then I hear that tone in her voice, like a tiny song—and I miss it so much.

"You should tell Arty," she says. "I think it'll help."

The words fly through me but don't connect. The song in her voice reminds me of a year ago, when Grampa died and I was pretty messed up. How Mom stayed up nights, sitting on the bed between my body and the wall, stroking my hair. She'd tell me all about Dad, and about good things they did together, when all I had ever heard before was so bad. There were good stories to tell. Sure, I don't remember them now, not a one, but her voice floated there above my comforter in that empty space. Kind of like a kid saying a prayer to God or something.

"No," Kurt says. His voice rises just loud enough for me to hear above a whooshing car. "If I told him, he'd only make it harder."

"I know I'm not the great communicator or anything, but I could talk to him," Mom says.

"I want to keep it a secret between us," Kurt says.

I strain to hear Mom's reply. It eases out in a breath like a light draft. "Honey," she says. "I'm proud of you just for trying. I always will be."

But "a secret between us" is all I hear. It's the only thing I remember. Everything else that came before just kind of vanishes.

I'm so mad, my eyes throb, and I feel light-headed as I get up and walk into the house. It's like sleepwalking in some dream. Light from the kitchen wavers on the dark hallway floor. I hear Mom and Kurt moving and murmuring, but I'm not paying attention. I'm busy tugging the physiology worksheet off my forehead to restart the bleeding. The gash will look worse that way.

The oven door hangs open, and Mom hunches next to it, an apron tied over her work clothes. She balances a casserole in one hand, and I can tell just by looking at it that dinner's gone cold. Kurt leans against the white wall with both hands. The radio on the counter plays an old James Taylor song, and at that second the electric timer on the counter starts to beep.

Mom sees me there with my bloody homework in my hand and the gash on my forehead. Her face wrinkles; she squeaks and crosses the room with her arms outstretched. "Baby, baby," she says, and cradles my head in her oven mitts. Over her shoulder I see Kurt, eyes slanted, a purple vein in his neck worming around under the skin. The timer beeps, over, and over, and over.

"What is this?" Mom says, smearing her thumb against my head. "What is this?"

"A cut, just a cut, Mom."

"It's all swollen up. Did someone cut you? Did you fall? You've got them all over you, baby. What happened?"

"Yeah, I fell," I say. "It was pretty stupid."

"Did someone do this to you?" she says, and then she remembers the oven mitts and flings them to the floor like she's a hockey player about to start pummeling. "Listen, Arty, did someone do this to you? You tell me. I'll take that principal apart so fast, he won't remember how to zip his own fly."

Kurt watches us, still pushing the wall over with all of his eight thousand pounds or so of muscle. The beeping goes on, but no one seems to care or notice.

"What are you looking at?" I say to him. "Don't you have zits to pick or something?"

Then, in three long strides, Kurt moves to the counter and swipes the timer from its spot by the microwave. He punches the button to kill the noise. I've never seen his face so red, even with all the pimples. And his eyes seem swollen. But swollen from what? Crying? No way.

Mom checks my whole head, from eyes and ears to nose and neck, pulling the skin, caressing. "We'll talk later, Kurt," she says. "Okay?" No doubt she wants to discuss their little conspiracy further.

"Whatever," Kurt says as he tosses the timer into the sink, where it starts to beep again. Then he leaves, just like I wanted him to.

And I'm sort of happy, which is a rare thing.

I do my homework and have dinner with Mom. We work together at the dining room table, she on her legal files and me on my advanced algebra. We take turns getting up to sharpen pencils. Mom turns up the radio when the songs she likes come on. They're almost always cheesy country crap, but they remind me of home. 'Cause we live in the country, and it's cheesy, and most of the time it's a pretty big load of crap.

At ten I kiss her on the cheek and gather my school stuff for the morning. I notice that she's written *Kurt Kurt Kurt* in the margins of an ink-smeared photocopy. When she asks me to refill her coffee, I pretend not to hear. Not tonight, lady.

Kurt-Kurt-Kurt can get your damn coffee.

A GROCERY STORY

I can go through the exact motions of this dream in my mind, and it has all the cool DVD features, like rewinding and jumping ahead frame by frame: Grampa clutches chest. Lady by canned tomatoes gasps, her mouth spreading like a growing stain. Dude in suit-and-tie steps back, spooked.

That was only a year ago, a time when Grampa fed the birds down the street at Shilling Park, instead of the worms in some cemetery in New York State. In the dream, as it was in life, he collapses in aisle seven at the Giant, dropping out of the motorized wheelchair, arms twitching. I know the exact tile on the store floor, its black scuff bruised on my brain like the soft spot of an apple. I spend nights seeing Grampa rolling back and forth, soaked in sweat, gurgling down deep in his throat.

I remember how I ran to the store manager and told him my grampa fell out of his chair. How I ran back and crouched close to Grampa's face, and held his hand and talked to him and told him he was the best grampa in the world and that I loved him and he was not allowed to die.

I was so stupid.

I stand in that spot now, right on that black-scuffed tile. They moved the canned tomatoes to aisle eleven last summer.

Grampa died last June. It all started here in aisle seven.

Grampa loved to price hunt. He even got one of those lame T-shirts that said BORN TO SHOP from a garage sale where the people were just giving stuff away for free. He took Kurt and me to the store when he could; I don't know why, really. He taught us how to hunt for bargains. He drove one of those little motorized carts with the basket on the front, and his oxygen canister had its own special hookup near the back wheels, secured by these stretchy rainbow straps. Kurt and I used to fight over the possible havoc we'd wreak behind the wheel of Grampa's Hombre 12 Motorized Support System.

The old guy would plop me in the basket in front

and scoot down each aisle like he was back in his Sherman tank, clobbering the grocery Nazis with an assortment of specialty coupons. The winding and unwinding sound of the motor, the smell of sweet aftershave on the handlebars, his hair like the guts of some emptied lint trap. It was perfect.

I still do most of the family shopping now. I dig the smells and the sounds, the misting of produce, and the bleeps of the register scanners.

It's Wednesday night, and I currently wrestle with the choice between flesh-colored Active-Stretch brand bandages and the generic store brand, with advanced skin-tone Fiberwear technology. I go for the generic store brand, of course, to help with family expenses, though once in my life I'd love to splurge on the cocoa sugar-frosted cereal with the singing monkey on the box. I move down the aisle with my wheeled dolly rolling behind me, one eye on the cosmetics shelves and the other on the list I've got wrapped around my finger. I follow grocery lists closely, like I'm a pirate with a treasure map, and this rack labeled FEMININE HYGIENE is my X marks the spot.

Mom prefers Always brand. Such a reassuring-sounding maxipad. Luckily, the bulk pack sits on the lowest shelf, within my reach. Buying Always makes me think of Mom, the way she emphasized *always* when she said she loved us. Dad far away in a stolen car, pursued by cops and lawyers by the freaking dozen. And Mom close by, saying over and over, "I love you. I'll *always* love you." Always. Such a reassuring word: *always*.

I reach out and take the white plastic handle. But when I pull back, the maxis don't move.

There is another hand.

I pull harder.

But when I look up, a cold burn cuts straight through my chest and makes my heart go brittle like a snow cone.

Leslie Dermott has my Always in her hand—Leslie Dermott in the flesh, standing at the FEMININE HYGIENE rack and holding a bulk box of maxipads. *My* bulk box of maxipads.

Leslie Dermott, who works the snow-cone machine that made my cherry heart.

I want to slather my face in zit concealer and shuffle off to hide among the deli meats. She hasn't caught on to me yet. Her face is buried in the pages of a book called *So You Want to Fly Balsa-Wood Gliders*. Together we tug the plastic Always handle until it stretches and begins to break. I can't bring myself to let go. Leslie's hair looks darker than usual—I think because it's wet—and she has it piled sloppily in the hood of a gray sweatshirt. The elastic around the waist must be shot, so the fabric billows loose, and it looks more like she's curled up in a cozy blanket than a shirt.

Then she notices me, and she smiles. It's her smile.

The one I see at school every day. No sharp edges, nothing scary, just gentle curves, like her body.

"Hi, Arty."

Holy crud. She knows my name.

I should not say a word. It will definitely come out as something rude or stupid or just really, really lame, and send her scurrying to seek cover behind the giant cheese wheels. Even as this rationalization kicks in, I feel my mouth begin to open. I lick my lips. Don't. Stop.

Then out it pops. "Hey, Leslie."

Where did that come from? Who authorized it? Was it too much, not enough?

"Are you here by yourself?" she says.

"Yeah." Good job, I tell myself; answer her questions. "Parents don't really do so much shopping." Right, keep it simple.

It blows me away how good she looks up close. As I talk she opens the Always package and whips out one of the white envelopes. She raises her eyebrows and pops the maxi into her purse, patting the brown leather with one hand. "Going to need that one later, if you get me," she says.

"Sure," I say. I'm trying to ignore what she just did and think about her looks. That's not a problem.

"There's nothing as irritating as getting your period on cram night," she says. "It's like having a hangover during midterms. It stinks." She keeps working that smile, her lips like pink cake frosting. "You shop alone, then?"

"Yup," I say, still not over the whole "period on cram night" thing.

"Why's that?"

"Mom's too busy, I think. And I kind of like it, you know. It's sometimes fun, in a weird way. I don't know." Stop picking your fingers! Look her in the eyes. Everyone always talks about eye contact.

"'Too busy,' huh?" she says. "You ever have trouble in the store, getting around and stuff?"

I knew it. Here it comes, the old "But, how can a little guy actually get around by himself?" scenario— an oldie but a goodie.

"What do you mean?" I say, baiting the hook.

She doesn't even flinch. "Being really small," she says. "It looks like it might be tough. You are kind of short, you know."

I laugh. I can't help it. For the first time I see the crop of freckles at the bridge of her nose, and I laugh again.

"What's so funny?" she says.

"You called me 'short,'" I say, covering my face with a sleeve. "No one's called me short since . . . hell, I don't know when."

It's true. People call me midget or shrimp or Willow or Lucky the Leprechaun or Mini-Me, but never "short." A doctor once said I was "stunted," which is a pretty mean thing to say.

I smile back at her for the first time. "I mean, think about it. You said I was 'kind of short,' and you said it in this way, like you were asking me if I'd ever noticed it or something. Yeah," I say, nodding excitedly, "I've noticed. All systems are a go."

"How old are you?" she says. "I've been meaning to ask."

Leslie Dermott has been meaning to ask me something. *Me.* I have been on her mind.

"I'm fourteen," I say.

"Seriously?" she says, jaw dropping. Then she shakes off the shock, and her eyes brighten. Wow. "But you didn't answer my first question," she says, cocking her head and spilling hair from her hood. "Do you have trouble shopping or not? Since you've already admitted you have one problem, now would be a good time to get some others off your chest. What do you think?"

Boy, does she flirt. I love this. I'm flirting. It's like zooming down a steep hill on a bike with no brakes.

"Oh sure, 'trouble,' yeah; it can be some trouble sometimes," I say. "You know, the hardest is picking out frozen foods. You may not have noticed, but they have these big heavy doors, and the things are suction sealed, like you're stuck on a space station or something. I've got to practically climb in the freezer to reach anything. So this one time when I was, like, eleven, one of those huge doors closed on me when I was inside. I was in the freezer for half an hour. I spent the whole time tapping on the glass in Morse code, waiting for some lady to wander by in search of Lean Cuisine."

A woman in a beret and pantsuit elbows past Leslie at the instant she giggles. It makes her do this cute hiccup thing and then kind of suck the giggle back in. I can't get over the sound, and I'm certain no one has ever made that noise before, ever. I love it. I want her to talk to me like that, in a secret language like the squeaks and clicks of dolphins. Words only for us.

"Well, it looks like you made it out okay," she says. "Who do we have to thank?"

"The butcher."

"You and he close now?"

"Yeah, sure, we borrow each other's clothes."

Reality strikes as she releases a full-blown belly laugh. This girl's face, a face I've dreamed about reaching up into the air above my bed and touching, floats inches from my own. The open package of Always hangs from her hand, and a slice of damp brown hair cups her chin. A scent of citrus, like an orange Popsicle, fills the small space between us, rising up from her tiny wrists, which stick out from her sleeves and tinkle with silver-and-turquoise bracelets. The jangling of the jewelry gets in on the sound, mixing with her giggles, and it's perfectly beautiful music.

I don't know how long we talk like this, but we have to step out of the way at least three times to let shopping carts squeeze past. I let my big mouth off its leash and feel it take off, dragging me with it. No more worries. Leslie loves what I have to say, and I don't even know what it is. Talking to her makes me feel weightless, not because I'm angry but because of something else.

She accidentally brushes my arm, as if to say: Who would have ever thunk it, the two of us? She's right. I don't know what I'm saying anymore, but it feels like we're trading secrets that we've kept only to ourselves for way too long.

AGAINST THE ROPES

 THE SCHOOL NEWSLETTER OF

THE FILLMORE HIGH SCHOOL BOXING TURTLES

"A turtle only makes progress when it sticks out its neck."
—Anonymous

WEEK OF MAY 16–22

🐢 Don't forget the schoolwide "Casino Night Party" (theme as of yet undetermined) on June 3rd. Become cooler to your classmates, because that's what really matters!

🐢 Sing Shakespeare's finest lines to the greatest music ever written, all while dressed in padding and multi-colored tights! *The Merry Wives of Windsor* is almost cast; hurry and try out this week. Juicy parts such as *the corpse* can still be yours.

🐢 Cut out the coupon on the back of page 5 for a free sundae from Viking Ice Cream, on Radar Run Road. "Viking, Your Ice Is Ours."

🐢 WOWEKAZAAM: For all your costume and party needs. If it's tight, we have it.

🐢 Stop by and chat with representatives from military schools and preparatory schools across the East Coast and New England. More than twenty institutions will be represented. Wednesday, 4:00 in the cafeteria. Those of you who have received special slips are required to attend and must bring a parent, guardian, or parole officer.

🐢 NEW: "Armageddon Thunder 3015" Tabletop Gamers Club, Mondays, during lunch in the library. Call Leslie: 579-9877.

Girls on Film

"S o, you want to go to a movie?" Leslie says into the phone.

"Is this Leslie?" My throat seems to shrivel up like a dried leaf. Am I still dreaming?

"It's not the Virgin Mary, if that's what you're thinking."

"What? Leslie, is that you?" I look around to track my mother's movements as she closes the fridge, gives me the eye, and then proceeds to the exercise bike, which she straddles in a single bound. She fires up a video of the streets of Shanghai.

It's Monday morning, five days after Leslie and I had our little rap beside the panty-shield shelf. Not that I'm counting.

"Of course, it's me, silly," she says. "You must need some coffee."

"It's early," I say, edging around the doorway and into the living room. I can't believe she's calling me. I didn't think we were listed in the phone book. I thought Mom had us taken off the list after Dad got out of prison and everything.

"So, are we going to the movies, or what?"

"We have school," I say. But I can tell she won't be stopped that easily.

"School will be there tomorrow," she says. "And Shadow-Puppet Club can wait."

"You're in Shadow-Puppet Club?" I say. "I didn't even know there *was* a Shadow-Puppet Club."

"I founded it," Leslie says. I can just imagine Leslie and a bunch of weirdos huddled around a flashlight and giggling, like girls on acid at a slumber party. "Oh, and you absolutely have to come to our performance over summer vacation."

"What, shadow puppets?"

"No, silly, Drama Club. I'm in that, too. We're doing Shakespeare this summer, and I'm one hundred percent psyched."

"Sounds great," I say.

"So, are we moviegoing, or what?" she says.

"What about your parents?" I say as I glance back into the kitchen and across to the back room. Mom slaloms in and out of bikes and scooters, scaring chickens. "Don't they care if you cut school?"

"They're in La Suisse for the month," she says. "You don't want me to call and interrupt happy hour, do you?" Her voice sounds rougher, more distracted. I know better than to miss such an open fly-ball opportunity.

"Movies it is," I say, as if I needed convincing.

Then, without any sort of warning, she screams into the receiver like someone's just broken into her house and is coming after her with a Cuisinart. "Holy crap!"

I yank my ear away.

Her shrieking fills the empty room. "Turn to channel seven. Now!"

I go into the family room at the front of the house and scoop the TV remote out from where it's wedged in the couch cushions. I pick a melted Junior Mint off buttons seven and eight, and then click on the power.

"As of yet there are no new leads," Wendy King says into her mike, standing like a cardboard cutout against the backdrop of my school. "I repeat, for those of you just joining us, there are no new leads in the Millie the Boxing Turtle case. However, Mayor Fitzgerald has issued a statement condemning the burglary, and has appealed to those responsible to surrender the high school monument to the authorities, assuring that a quick resolution will insure gentler consequences."

I click from channel to channel, but they all show the same thing: a file photo of a feisty stone turtle with boxing gloves. Chet Krieger of channel three cuts to live cameras on the scene—six of them to be exact, dynamic angles of the same empty stone pedestal.

"Oh, man," I say.

"Isn't it amazing?" Leslie says. I stand there, stunned, and watch as a policeman chases a pair of arguing camera guys off Millie's lonely perch, rolling his sleeves up before stalking out of the frame. A few dropped flowers already color the spot where she stood. I'm definitely awake now.

"I'll be by in ten minutes," Leslie says.

"I didn't know you could drive," I say. "You're sixteen?" Hopefully, younger girls aren't as age sensitive as older women.

"I have a car, don't I? Of course, I'm sixteen. That's what happens when you spend years climbing mountains and scuba diving instead of sitting in classrooms."

"What, you get a car?"

"No. You end up behind with all your school credits. Duh. And trust me—I've been to schools all over the place. Bali or Bolivia, it's always the same thing."

"I'll take your word for it," I say.

"Ten minutes," she reminds me, and promptly hangs up.

I don't leave the room right away after turning off

the TV. I spend some time staring out the window. Clouds everywhere. Not a day to be outside.

I feel bad for old Millie. She never hurt anybody. All she ever did was give a scared midget a place to hide. I try not to let the news ruin my morning. Instead, I picture Leslie with wet hair over one eye and her back against row after row of hemorrhoid creams. The image gets me through breakfast and into a set of clean clothes.

Leslie does have a car, a pristine white Volkswagen Jetta, with a hologram bumper sticker that says PRINCESS in blue prisms.

After a long breakfast, we pull into the mall parking lot. The first drops of rain strike the cement as we step from the car, and they build to a downpour by the time we reach the theater lobby. The world on the other side of the windows darkens to a charcoal color, and wet streaks ooze down the glass.

The Cinema at Southworth Mall doesn't get much business at eleven on a Monday morning. A group of old guys from a nursing home shuffle by the box office and fork over money for a movie called *This Is the First Day of the Rest of Your Death*. The walls shake with every clap of thunder. The few poor fools who just bolted quickly inside for coffee from Java Jackpot gaze out longingly at their cars. Nobody around here seems to have heard of an umbrella.

As I stand there going over the movie choices, Leslie lets out a squeal of joy and rushes toward the doors. A tiny speck of a girl stands on the lobby carpet, flicking rain off a flowered umbrella. The girl fails to crack a smile as Leslie approaches, and she mechanically pats her back with a flat hand when Leslie sucks her into an excited embrace. Leslie guides the girl toward me, that huge Leslie grin pasted across her face.

I can't believe this. This girl actually wears one of those old-fashioned maid costumes, like with powder blue frills and a white apron across the front—everything. I can't help but notice how her green eyes shine even brighter than Leslie's, which are famous school-wide for their fluorescence. This girl, whoever she is, has positively glow-in-the-dark-watch eyes—unbelievable, electrical.

"This is Camilla," Leslie says.

"Hi, Camilla," I say. I wave at her, though I'm close enough to shake her hand. I look like a mental patient on a field trip.

"Hello," Camilla says with a jumbled accent, and she reaches out and shakes my hand for me. The three of us laugh awkwardly, and Leslie wrings her hands together, the happy chaperone.

We get tickets for a foreign movie called *The Denouncement of the Oyster* and merge with the line at the snack bar. I would have rather seen the blockbuster

Superconductor, with Drake Flaunton, the action star. But I guess when you see movies with a girl, you see what *she* wants. I don't seem to have Dad's knack with the ladies, which in his case lasted just long enough for him to empty their purses and swipe their car keys.

Camilla pokes on the glass candy counter, directing the attendant to the supply of Baby Ruths. A long braid of black hair rests between her tiny shoulders. It reminds me of one of those dangling cords that people tug in old movies to summon a butler. Camilla's really pretty, not a model but a girl you could stop on the street to compliment, and who would be cool about it. And those wacky eyes.

"This film's Chinese," Leslie says as she orders a box of pretzel bites. "I've been wanting to see it for days."

Camilla works with two different theater clerks, stockpiling junk food. A chubby one in a paper hat heaps about eight boxes of candy onto a tray alongside a jumbo tub of popcorn drenched with butter that looks like hair conditioner.

"I've never heard of it," I say to Leslie, distracted. I surprise myself by saying this next bit to Camilla, who doesn't even turn around. "What's it about?"

"She hardly speaks any English," Leslie says. "Don't even try. You'd be better off talking to a wall."

It's a terrible thing to say. I clear my head and try to pretend it didn't happen. "Do you guys see a lot of movies?" I say. But it's too late. Leslie's comment lingers in the back of my brain like a bad taste in the mouth.

Oblivious, Leslie digs in her purse for a piece of scrap paper for her used gum. I watch. Bills wallpaper the inside, and I'm talking big bills—twenties and fifties.

"All the time," Leslie says. "Last month we saw *Intéressant,* a French film about a cheese farm."

"A 'cheese farm'?"

"Yeah. It was a murder mystery."

"Sounds mysterious," I say. "So how long have you two been friends?"

Leslie breaks into minor hysterics, laughing as she shows our tickets to the usher and stuffs both stubs into her pocket. "We're not friends, Arty," she says. "She's my maid." The terrible thing she said bobs back to the surface.

They haven't yet dimmed the lights in the theater, and the few people lame enough to come see *The Denouncement of the Oyster* stand in the aisles discussing *Intéressant,* the last movie any of them saw. Leslie and I sit in the very front row, and Camilla sits right behind us. She sets up shop with candy in the seats to her left and right.

"This film is set in ancient China," Leslie says, squishing up against my arm. "It tells the story of a family feud over a magic oyster that is said to charm fishing boats."

"Who wants to watch a movie about ancient China?" I say. "Especially about a fight over a clam. I could see that at Long John Silver's." I can be pretty funny when I want to be.

"I've been to China," Leslie says. "I traveled some of it on horse, and then other times on a train. We even did Hong Kong by yacht, in style."

"Really? Wow."

"I've been all over. Six continents."

I have to admit, I'm impressed. I've only been to one continent: whichever one this is.

My ass aches, and I fidget in my seat for a better position. I don't think theater owners developed springy audience chairs with freaks like me in mind. The air-conditioning must be on full blast, because my arm hairs stand up on end. "I don't like the movies," I say. The truth is that I probably haven't been to one in years.

"Why not? They're great," Leslie says. "Have a pretzel bite." The dough turns spongy and cold the second it hits my mouth. A ripple of indigestion wiggles through me.

"I just don't like them."

"You don't look so hot," Leslie says. "Are you okay?"

Where would I even start? The whole theater

seems to be going black, not like it's supposed to but in a weird way, like a gaping mouth or an open grave or something. A chilly sweat pops up on my neck, and I wipe it away with my sleeve.

"What's wrong? Tell me."

"Nothing. You'll think I'm a loser." I jerk my seat back and forth, and try to get comfortable until a metal bolt rolls out and clanks to the floor. I look at Leslie. "What I mean is that you'll think I'm *more* of a loser than you probably already do."

"I won't laugh. I promise." I'm really digging her green cat-eyes.

"Fine, fine," I say. "I don't like the dark, okay. I'm not afraid of it, but it makes me uncomfortable. I don't know, like claustrophobic. Like if something happens, I won't know how to get out." She listens with no expression. "Does that make any sense?"

I expect her to ask me why, but instead she picks salt off a pretzel bite and sighs when it falls in the lap of her expensive pants.

"You don't need to tell me everything," she says. Her hand lowers down onto mine, and it descends slowly, like an elevator you've been waiting for forever. She sets her head on my shoulder, which has to be hard on her neck because I'm so much shorter than she is, but she rests it there, anyway. I'm afraid to move, even to so much as inhale.

A slide show starts, ads for local businesses, each image as huge as a billboard: optician, local spa, gift certificates, NO TALKING, HEARING DEVICES AVAILABLE, self-help guru, TURN OFF CELL PHONES, and back to the optician. Next come slides for favorite movie quotes and "Rising Stars of Hollywood," intermixed with warnings that some guy with a tin can is going to gouge us for charity money at the end of the movie. I listen to Camilla scarf a box of Raisinets, and when she finishes that she proceeds with an assault on her jumbo tub.

I feel like saying one more thing, so I do. "I'm kind of a midget," I tell Leslie. For some reason it feels like I'm confessing a crime, like I should feel guilty about all of it.

"I don't think of you like that," Leslie whispers. Her breath smells like a margarita and what I think might be lipstick.

Music swells and the commercials begin. Camilla sticks a finger in my back. "Shut up, please," she whispers in halting English.

It's the best thing I've heard all day.

I go to the restroom six times during the movie, just to go from the darkness to the lights. But each time I return to my seat, because in the darkness waits Leslie Dermott—and some things are worth coming back for.

THE ASS KICKER

Later that night we sit on the roof of Leslie's Jetta and slurp ice cream out of a long paper dish.

As usual Viking Ice Cream teems with teenagers. The small parlor sits a couple of blocks north of Fillmore High and shares land with the community college's radio telescope observatory. And despite Viking Ice Cream's popularity, its parking lot is rarely full. Kids pull their cars under the trees by the field next door and park near the hulking radio telescope dishes. The dishes make the world seem bigger, or the rest of us seem smaller. They're so huge one might just snap free of its base and trap all us kids underneath, like flies under a teacup.

"I'm going to tell you," I say at last.

"Fine," Leslie says. She licks a drop of whipped cream from a bright red lip. This is how I want to tell secrets. With a girl, and whipped cream, and the chirp of crickets.

"We'd been pretty good friends since we were kids," I tell her. "That's why it was so weird. Maybe he was holding things in for a while. I don't know. But by then he was super freaking big. So when he came at me that day, I couldn't fight back, or do anything, really. It was June seventh.

"He stuffed me into this chest we had down in the basement of our old house, this expensive antique thing that Dad had left behind. Kurt actually used the key and everything. He locked me in there, in the dark. And the creep left me there. Inside that box for I don't remember how long. I think he even forgot he'd done it, 'cause the next day he opened it and I was still there. It wigged him out so bad, he took off. He avoided me for weeks afterward. That was when he started disappearing."

I don't mention how Kurt found me lying in my own piss. Or how Mom was on some "business trip" with her bosses and didn't come back when she said she would. How I was all alone against him.

Viking Ice Cream is known for three ice-cream specialties: How I Learned to Love the Bomb (a banana split with five bananas), Please Clean Up After

Your Dog (a fudge sundae with three kinds of nuts), and the Ass Kicker (five flavors chosen at random by the spin of a large cardboard wheel above the counter). We ended up with bubble gum, pistachio nut, café au lait, peanut-butter cup, and raspberry mint chip.

Leslie listens, licking her spoon clean. Mint chips dot her chin, though she doesn't know it, and peanut-butter cup stains the wrinkles of her mouth, and it gives her a messy-little-kid look that I love. The college girls in the car next to us play Simon and Garfunkel so low, it's only a mumble. They sit and smoke in their pajamas, their How I Learned to Love the Bombs melting, their faces creased with exhaustion like smashed couch cushions. Two of them talk about the weird kidnapping of that turtle statue over at Millard Fillmore High. "Totally creepy," they agree.

Leslie pushes a blob of pistachio nut my way with her spoon. She just looks so good all the time. I'm even over how she acted like a bitch at the theater, with that comment about Camilla. Well, I'm almost over it.

"Did you make that story up?" Leslie says, a smile waiting to bloom across her face.

Make it up? "Nothing but the truth," I say. "Scout's honor. Why?"

She smiles, but small, carefully. "Well, you know, you can be kind of intense."

Intense, huh. I guess that's better than short.

"Sometimes I overcompensate," I say. "Kind of for everything."

Blinking with sleepiness, she mulls my words, and then finally licks her spoon again. "I feel so bad for you," she says. "I didn't even know you had a brother. It makes me want to know how your whole relationship affected him, you know? Have you ever wondered that?"

My brother isn't affected by anything. And no, I've never wondered. "He's nothing but a blob," I point out.

"You don't think he took that turtle, do you?" she says out of the blue. Funny, never in a million years would I have thought that. Until now.

I push the melted pistachio nut back in her direction. "No more talking," I say. "Eat your Ass Kicker."

DRIED

The chirp of the crickets along my street tapers off as quickly as it started. It fades as my fingertips brush the doorknob, leaving the skin tingling on the back of my neck.

It's been that kind of night. Like life in the movies, cinematic and full of amazing endings. We held hands. We talked until ten and made sailor hats out of the real estate section of the newspaper. We laughed all the time.

Leftovers from the light rain drop from gutters and awnings, and trash can lids make tiny puddles swimming with leaves, seeds, and bits of cut grass. On nights like this you never see anybody, and that's okay with me. No dogs bark. No cars pass. All you hear is the crackle of the crickets. I feel alive, big as the Empire State Building, giant like a California redwood.

The screen door clatters against the doorframe, but there's no one home to hear it. In the kitchen the refrigerator buzzes and the portable radio fizzes in and out of range. The living room sits still and pink in the light glowing through the curtains. It makes me think of Christmas, how the dying red flames from the fireplace tint the whole room with holiday colors.

On Christmas Eves past, Grampa would come home from the store with last-second gifts and find me still up and waiting in my footy pajamas. He'd shake the minisnowballs off his boots and then sweep me up in his sandpaper hands, inching me down over the top of the Christmas tree like I were an astronaut fixing some satellite. I would aim, reach out, and work our paper angel right onto that tip.

There are no logs in the fireplace now. Not in May. I'd love to tell my grampa about Leslie Dermott. I know he'd say something clever about how I pulled that angel right down off the top of the Christmas tree and took her out for ice cream. He'd be proud of me, no doubt.

On my way out of the kitchen, I put the radio out of its misery. I feel like I'm high, like it's about time to mix my medication, because, who knows, maybe tonight's the night—to feel lucky, to grow.

I get up the first couple of steps before I hear the sound. I hesitate, one foot levitating, when I hit the top stair. A throttled choke comes from down the second-floor hallway. My heart starts beating faster. Each step I take, the more the sound makes sense to me—and sounds strangely familiar.

It's crying, and it's coming from Kurt's bedroom.

I picture Mom after Grampa died, all those nights. How she wobbled against the reception table at the funeral home. Or the times after Dad split, when I found her wet face glued to the paperwork on her desk. A lot of times she didn't even get up in the morning. She stayed at home and slept for hours on the couch in her leotard.

This crying sounds like that, weak and broken. Like Grampa's funeral all over again.

I rush into the room to comfort her. But it isn't Mom.

Kurt sobs so hard into his pillow that he might just want to blow a hole out the other side. His back jerks up and down, a muscle spasm in blue jeans and a T-shirt. The phone lies in pieces on the floor.

I'm shocked Kurt's even at home. I feel ambushed, but I'm too dazed to move, too stupid to back away slowly from the wild animal.

As I stand there, Kurt lifts his head from the bed and

looks at me. "Go away!" The scream doesn't even seem meant for me. He roars it at the few empty feet between us. His eyes bulge, bloodshot. Snot runs down his neck and across the muscles on his chest. Sometimes I fantasize about having that strong body, wonder what it would be like to see it in the mirror.

"What's wrong, you get dumped?" I say. My voice comes out sharp and cold, like I just pulled a knife.

"Leave me alone!" he says again. He swings one huge arm out and catches me napping. Sharp fingernails scrape across the bridge of my nose, and I stumble backward.

"They teach you that move at the zoo?" I say.

"Shut up," he says. In between gasps his voice grows calm.

"You talking to Koko over at the monkey house?" I say. "Did she find another alpha male to replace you?"

"I'm gonna kill you," he says.

"Or maybe I've got the wrong ape. Not Koko . . ." And I let the name work its way slowly across my lips. I actually enjoy the delivery. "Mary Fielder, maybe?"

The name—and my knowledge of it—seems to sting Kurt as if I'd slapped him. We gaze at each other, and I see in his wild eyes what's coming.

I spin and dive for the empty hallway. But my short legs catch on a stack of books sitting on the floor, and

I clear the doorway tripping, miles to go to the stairs and to safety.

I feel Kurt's nails carve into my arms, and I know he's squeezing as hard as he can, and it kills.

"What'd you hear?" he says.

"Crying," I say. "Calling for Mommy." It's all I can manage. The fingers clamped into my arms feel like hot matches sunken in the skin.

"Piece of—" Kurt says, but interrupts himself as he initiates takeoff, hoisting me like Grampa did at Christmas.

I see carpet, floor, and ceiling, picture frames, light fixtures—all spinning as he flings me around. I'm going to die; I just know it. So I start kicking. I channel every bit of energy into my stumpy legs and scream at the top of my lungs. I will not go quietly. Not this time.

"You're dead!" he says.

Then I kick him in the nose.

I have never *really* hit my brother in my entire life. But in this instant of terror, my shoe connects with something solid that gives under the pressure, and Kurt snaps back, surprised, as blood speckles the drywall.

With a howl he hoists me up over his head, and I think he's actually going to hurl me down the stairs. Instead, he charges down to the first floor with me above him like a hang glider. The second his socks hit the wood floor, he slips, and we smash against the entryway table, spraying a cloud of orange potpourri into the air. I scramble loose.

"No!" I say, straining for the front door.

Then I'm back in Kurt's grown-up hands, and I smell his stink around me, a stench like the sink disposal. I thrust out for anything to grab and find his hair. Then I yank until I've got enough for the worst toupee ever. But he won't let go, doesn't loosen his grip for a second.

He carries me down through the finished basement and into the utility room. There a metallic banging smothers his clomping footsteps. The groan of the washing machine.

No, wait. The dryer.

"Kurt! Please!"

I open my eyes in time to see the dark hole gaping. I don't kick or scream or punch. The fear overwhelms me, and every one of my muscles seems to die a quick death, leaving me limp and helpless.

I bang my head on the rim of the dryer as he tosses me in. He only grunts. That's it. Like I'm just a bag of trash he's winging to the side of the road.

It's my last frantic thought as the door slams shut behind me.

SWEET BiG FEELiNG

It's still early morning when I find sweet freedom. Then I go for my medication.

Why hello there, bedroom closet; it's me, Arty. Oh, look at this, a tape measure, just sitting here stuck to the wall. Let's give it a try, shall we; see what the old boy has to say.

What's that? Four feet two inches tall? You don't say.

Cartridges. Mitten. Needles. Cotton balls. Generic Active-Stretch bandages.

I sit in the desk chair to collect my rage, breathing it in slowly like it's poison gas. "You know the drill," I say. "Think of something." My voice leaks out through clenched teeth. My hands shake from exhaustion.

My right thigh has gotten kind of lumpy around the injection spot, as it does every so often, so I switch to the left and get ready to jab. At the last second, I grab my shirt and pull it up and sink the needle right into my abdomen. It hurts. God, it hurts. But it's good. Just another cut, or bruise, or scrape to survive.

Think of something.

I think of that face. His face. His face on that night a few years ago.

I think of how his face twisted when the latch of the chest came up and the lid flew open. It was the first time I recognized fear on my brother's face.

I had burst into tears, so happy to see him, to see anybody. But I was scared the hell out of my mind, too, because I didn't have a clue as to what he might do to me next. I remember the stench of the basement mildew, still so much better than the puddle of stale pee I'd spent the night in.

Kurt came to his senses, or at least remembered how to take control, and grabbed my hair.

"You tell Mom about this and I'll make your life hell," he said.

I didn't say anything. Too busy crying like a psycho, I guess.

Will I say something this time? This time I got out. That's right. He pushed a dresser in front of the dryer door to keep me in. But I kicked that freaking door until I thought my knees would buckle, and I escaped. He couldn't keep me locked up. He can't keep me quiet.

I can hardly feel the needle now. It's like a snow-flake just landed there and is beginning to melt. A cool, spreading sensation on my stomach.

I think it's hate I feel.

I'm going to make him wish we'd never been born.

REVENGE IS A DISH
BEST SERVED BALD

Police officers and reporters mingle in a horde on the school lawn, but I don't care. It's hard to tell the difference between the cops and the journalists. Together they all canvass the area, looking for clues or interviews as cameramen zoom in on the sign that says: A TURTLE ONLY MAKES PROGRESS WHEN IT STICKS OUT ITS NECK. Normally I'd be standing by myself in the back of the crowd, making smart-ass cracks about the idiots who always jump and wave behind the reporter in hope of getting caught on TV.

But not today.

I stand in Tuesday-morning foot traffic in the front hall of school. Kids jostle around and by me like the rapids of a river.

Between the principal's office and the nurse's office stands a red door. It leads to the basement. Teachers call the tunnels under the school the arts wing. Some kids call them that, too, but usually as a joke. Down there is where all the hoods go to class—the junkies, punks, and felons—all of those misfits who barely qualify to be in public school in the first place. Rumor has it that big trouble brews down under while the rest of us go about our daily lives, and trouble is just what I'm looking for.

I don't want to hang in the hall too long; hanging around is a sure sign you're thinking about snagging the free condoms off the nurse's desk. So I take a deep breath and grab the red doorknob and pull. A trickle of steam claws its way around the doorframe, and it carries the smells of burned hair and Jolly Ranchers.

I plunge down into the fog. A pipe clunks in the mist overhead, then starts to groan as I feel my way down the crumbly staircase. When I reach the bottom step, I find an archway opening to a corridor of uneven cinder-block walls. Magazine collages blanket the corridor and the low ceiling. Clippings of babies and flowers and fashion models and car wrecks hide every bare inch of surface. Photos of lions feasting on bloody antelope gaze down at me as I pass.

The first door I come to sticks, locked. The next door opens up to brown sawdust swirling in the heat and blowing across the unfinished floor to the grinding shriek of table saws. A bunch of kids with puffy, shredded-wheat–looking hair carve blocks of wood at their workbenches. Pools of paint dry in the cracks of the floor. A girl in one corner leans alone over a pedestal, working a pedal, squishing clay between her hands, and singing in a wispy voice.

The boy I'm looking for is not here, so I try the next door.

Walking into this room is like stepping back in time into one of those old industrial photographs where all the guys have buff greasy bodies and swing giant hammers as they build some future society. Students drill through sheets of tin, making a sound like thousands of zippers being wrenched up and down too fast. Above me silver air ducts dangle with mobiles that turn in the weak wind of a fan. Gears twist and blowers send shoots of greasy smoke toward the plumbing, which is visible through cracks in the corrugated ceiling.

As I cross the threshold, an arc of sparks spurts up from a saw and sails toward my face. I'm doomed until a pair of warm gloved hands pull me from the line of fire and into a safe space behind the drafting boards.

A girl bends down on one knee to look me in the eyes through her safety goggles. Her hair is wound up in a dingy ponytail. I recognize her as the girl I call

Oil Change, the same girl who gave me that stupid brochure, like, a week ago. Some kind of sludge dribbles down one ear as she mouths a bunch of words I can't hear over the clanking. I don't call her Oil Change for nothing.

"What are you doing here?" she shouts. "This place is dangerous, all right." She wears baggy overalls with stains ground into the knees. A blood-soaked bandage peeks out from under her left workman's glove. Pinned to it shines a red letter *A* pin, like an open wound that dried.

"I want to see Kerouac," I say. She smells like a flower shop under all that grime. "Is he here?"

"Who?"

Then I remember my classification system, my code names, and realize she doesn't know who I'm talking about. I struggle to think of Kerouac's real name, and I have no idea. Have I ever even heard it?

"Let me guess," she says, patting a wrench against her palm. "You're looking for Jack?"

The name doesn't set off any alarms, but I nod anyway. She seems to understand.

"Is he expecting you?" she says.

I didn't know I needed to make an appointment. Remembering how it felt struggling in the total darkness of the dryer, spine on the cold metal slats, I actually bark at her. "I need to talk to him."

"Are you Arty?" she says. I'm surprised she knows me, and even more so when she takes off the glove on her good hand and we shake, like we're heads of state or something.

"I'm Rose Purdy," she says. "I'm Jack's girlfriend." I admit that I didn't expect this curveball. From the first time I saw him, Kerouac was the last person I'd expect to have a girlfriend. The last person other than me, that is. Rose pulls an extra pair of goggles off the horizontal rack and hands them to me. "Here," she says. "So you don't get shavings in your eyes. They can blind you if you're not careful."

She leads me behind towering stacks of scrap to an alcove where four boys and a girl sit hunched around a wobbly table. They play the card game Uno with a creased, dirty deck, slugging Pins & Needles brand ginger ale from stolen cafeteria cups. The empty two-liter bottle serves as an ashtray. Cat Ballou, the girl, sleeps behind her sunglasses, her face smashed in an open trigonometry textbook. Behind her Arachnid and Sirloin still fight over a rule from their stupid Dungeon Master's manual, hardly paying attention to their Uno cards. From the way it sounds, it's the same rule they argued about the day of the penny parade.

There, with his back to the wall, relaxes Kerouac, the man I've come to see.

"And that's why Dietrich will drop out," a buff black

kid I call Ice Pick says to the other card players. He rocks back on his chair legs and gnaws at a candy bar.

"Not if he fails the fitness test," Kerouac says, elbowing Arachnid, who puts down the Dungeon Master's manual and passes Kerouac a piece of paper. Kerouac scans the typed sheet and signs it several times, then hands it back. Little oval reading glasses balance on the end of his beaky nose. He pulls them off to rub his eyes. "I'm telling you," he says, "failing the fitness test is our in, man. Dietrich will show up faster than food poisoning."

"Whatever. Fail this," Ice Pick says, giving Kerouac the finger and dropping a *Draw Four* card onto the Uno pile.

Kerouac takes the cards and grumbles, rebuilding his hand as he glances over and sees Rose and me coming. "Arty!" he says. "What's up, my man?" He pats me on the back. Ice Pick and Arachnid give me the once-over.

"I need your help," I say to Kerouac. I can see every one of his cards as he plots his next move.

"What kind of help?" He raises an eyebrow at Ice Pick as he fingers the bent corners of a *Reverse* card. "I'm always glad to help dudes who need it."

"I need to get even with someone," I say.

"With who?"

"My brother." It squeaks out. "I want him to leave me alone."

"Man, whose brother doesn't treat 'em like crap?" Kerouac says. Ice Pick snorts and throws a *Draw Two* on the table, and then he downs a big old swig from his puke-yellow plastic cafeteria cup and wipes his lips on the front of his shirt. He burps an obscenity and grins with a mouthful of really crooked teeth. This kid's got the same good manners as my charming brother.

"Listen," I say. "I'm sick of it." The words leap out of me, and I chuck my safety goggles at the middle of the table. They clear the Uno discard stack and sail into a box of ball bearings across the room. The rage floods through me, like the flow of my hormone, a genuine surge of power. I could take them all on at once. "I can't stand it anymore!"

Kerouac bites his lip and nods. "It's about time," he says. He draws a cigarette with a gold tip from a fancy box in his jacket pocket. Rose leans across the table and lights the tip with a soldering iron.

"You think I can help you because I'm a punk?" Kerouac says. I wouldn't have put it that way, but yes, that's what I think. So much for my poker face.

"I hear stuff all the time," I say. "Not that I want to know."

"You're right," Kerouac says. "I'm not as bad as all that. But I have to keep up my image, you know. It throws people off my scent. It gives me room to work."

"What kind of work?" I say.

"Listen, brother," he says. "I'm a guy who cares. All most of us want is to get by around here, and give ourselves and our friends some space." He blows a funnel of smoke out of his nostrils and looks at me with eyes that never seem to focus, like he's staring at someone behind me instead of at me.

"You don't know what I'm talking about, do you?" he says. "Then it sounds like we still got some secrets that work."

"Whatever," I say, the heat and grinding starting to wear at my skull. "Can you help me?"

"Tell him about Ruparel," Rose says, and it comes out almost like a nag.

"Can we trust him?" Ice Pick says.

"Sure, we can trust him," Kerouac says. "Right, Arty-man?"

I don't know the answer. Part of me wonders if this should go any further. Just coming down here must have proved something about me, about what I can do if I'm pushed far enough.

Kerouac waits, and then he stops smiling. He leans forward in his chair, neck tensing with knots of pale skin. Suddenly that folded and stained copy of *On the Road* that he always keeps on him is in his hand, and he flips through the pages with a thumb. His eyes grow a little wider, a little more intense. "You know James Ruparel, right?" he says. "That transfer kid, the senior, played hockey for a year till he got booted 'cause of grades?"

"I think I know him." I imagine the smiley kid in the denim jacket who's always blabbing about the Columbus Blue Jackets. My name for him is Stanley Cup.

"Well, his dad pounds on him, dude," Kerouac says. "He beats the kid like a goddamn drum. Jim hasn't studied a single night in the last eight months. His grades slipped, and he's freaking, you know, because that's all he's got to get him out of this trench. So what do we do? We help Jim out. We pick up the slack."

With his empty hand, Kerouac scratches Arachnid's head, and the two of them resemble an ugly mutt and its master. "This bitch's got the next two weeks of Ruparel's homework right there," he says. He points to Arachnid's backpack, which leans against the desk leg. "Finals, too. Exams and every damn thing."

"And it's good," Arachnid says, nodding with something like pride.

"We provided the best in recycled and original schoolwork," Kerouac says. "And have you heard? Ruparel's got a clean ride up north to Minnesota this fall. Home free, Arty-man. No more trophies across the face for Jimbo. He's on his own, and we've been happy to help."

"He just wants to help people," Sirloin says, waving his last card. "By the way, Uno, suckers." His red hair twinkles with metal shavings. The tip of Rose's soldering iron hisses and gives off squiggles of steam.

"So you want to get your brother?" Kerouac says.

"Yeah."

"Then you've come to the right place. Kurt Moore, right? Fraternal twin? Likes shooting hoops after midnight? Lactose intolerant?"

"You know him?" I say.

"What do *you* think?"

The kids look at me, not speaking, listening to the shuffle of cards in Kerouac's fingers. He moves the cards in and out of his hands effortlessly, then fans them, flips them out, and fires them across the table.

"So," he says with a smile, "you playing?"

CAMP KEROUAC

A lone figure stands in the purple midnight shadows. One arm hangs out crooked, swinging a lantern that shines a single star of light over the matted grass. It's amazingly dark. Like a tanker wrecked at thirty thousand feet and chocolate-coated everything.

Kerouac wears a trench coat over a Dead Kennedys T-shirt. A Cleveland Indians baseball hat hides his bald head. He doesn't say hi, but swings the lantern toward the street that runs alongside the factory, where a row of houses continues to the end of the block. Some are abandoned and some aren't, but it's hard to tell the difference. This is the far east end of Old Quarry Road, past the quarry, past anything resembling civilization. Only cows out here, cows and quiet.

"That's my place," Kerouac says. "The one with the purple window shaped like a diamond. My dad works with glass. I helped him make that one when I was a kid. Pretty cool, huh?"

I always wondered about that one window, and who could possibly live in that clunky old place. "Yeah," I say, more impressed than I thought I'd be. *My* dad jacked Mom's Pontiac and stuck up a Rite Aid for a case of beer. Compared to that, anything is an improvement.

Even when I was a tiny kid visiting Grampa over the summers, I always imagined what it would be like to grow up in that house with the purple-diamond window, the dump across the street from the abandoned Snud bottling plant. Kerouac's house is in worse shape than the others, if that's possible. Every one of them is flat, drab, and saggy in the roof. Snud bottled all the classics here, everything from Zocko! to Pip-Pop.

"Follow me," Kerouac says.

He takes off, bent at the waist, a palm holding his hat to his head, clanking the lantern back and forth like a gravedigger. It feels strange to be here. My anger has died a bit since I went to Kerouac on Tuesday. Even so, I tug my hood over my head, hunker down, and follow. What have I got to lose?

With those long legs he easily outdistances me. I

manage to keep him in sight as we slosh through puddles of muck and trip over rusty wire. The moon comes out from behind a cloud bank and steams in the sky, ducking in and out of darkness like it's in a shooting gallery. At last rectangular formations grow bold against the night, and I can see how they form a small city below the ancient water tower that has the words SNUD KNOWS FIZZ stenciled on one side. All of it rings bells in my memory. Sounds and smells. I haven't been here in so long. Dogs bark, tucked away in far neighborhoods, and I smell the faint aroma of burning wood and weenies.

Kerouac stops under a corrugated awning to catch his breath. He pulls a cigarette from a pocket and taps it on his index finger. He offers me one, but I decline.

I try to get my bearings, which is tough since I haven't been to the old plant in years, not since before Dad left. To our right stands a wooden gatehouse with a padlock on the door, and an up-and-down bar that once stopped cars from coming up the drive. Behind it a gravel path leads off into the woods. The scene looks familiar, like an out-of-focus photo. Then it comes back to me.

This is where Grampa used to park the truck. Right here next to this wooden shack and its security bar. Sometimes we even ate lunch in the old shack when it rained, back when there wasn't a lock on the door.

It was Grampa's way to make use of everything. He always took us to the factory to search for junk he could clean up and put back out in the world. Like cool bits of metal for trinkets and jewelry, or classic pop bottles he could polish and put on the kitchen windowsill, where they'd catch the light and throw all sorts of colors. Like the sink-drain amulet I made Mom.

But we always came during the day, which made a big difference. I remember all the charred furniture littering the curbs, the delivery trucks riding high on blocks, and the skeletal warehouses like tombs in the empty fields.

Kurt and I used to love picking through the ruins.

The dilapidated guard shack leans like a drunk about to keel over. It's really kind of a sad scene. A faint orange light burns inside it, shining out from under the door crack.

"What's that light?" I say. Maybe it's a watchman or something.

"You don't need to worry about that," Kerouac says, patting me on the shoulder. "We share our space from time to time. It's hard to find privacy in a town this small."

Suddenly Kerouac bursts from under the awning and runs crouching along the wall of the closest warehouse, and I rush to catch him. His steps slow as he nears a cer-

tain window well, one that drops into the ground between a pair of boarded-up delivery doors. Then he dips
to one knee and sets the lantern in the mud.

His arm darting out like a cobra, Kerouac grabs my
wrist, making my heart jump wildly against my ribs. I
don't move a muscle, and he gently places my hand on
the thick metal bars covering the sunken window,
helping me feel my way around.

I can feel that most of the bars have been hacked off
at the bottom to leave a hole and a series of jagged
points. "Abracadabra," Kerouac whispers. I can tell he's
smiling in the darkness.

He releases my wrist, grabs the lantern, and then
slides through the wall like a ghost. *Abracadabra*. Just
like that.

I crouch alone in the cloudy moonlight. Damn it
all. There's nothing I can do but follow the glow of the
lantern.

I get down on all fours and duck my head, shim-
mying past the razor edges. There's a steep drop, and I
touch down on a cement floor that's so cold I can feel
it through my shoes. Kerouac's footsteps echo off to my
right. I feel the wall behind me, and guide my way
from cobweb to cobweb along the moldy brick and
mortar. He left me here. I know it. It's all just some big
practical joke. Bastard.

Then the lights come on.

Weak bulbs swinging from wires fizzle to life one by one by one. I hear gasps. And when my eyes adjust, I see about twenty kids lounging around the open warehouse on filthy mattresses with the springs poking out. They seem to release a collective sigh of relief when they see Kerouac, and uncover hidden bonfires that crackle in bulk-sized fruit cocktail cans. Around them are hulks of conveyor machines with their snapped canvas belts lying in bundles like strings of dried toothpaste. Blobs of deformed aluminum make the ground look spotted with fillings from a mouthful of enormous teeth. Ancient glass sculptures gleam from shelves and spots on the planked floor, bottling experiments gone horribly wrong. From an empty wall, a giant billboard shouts: SNUD SUPPORTS OUR BOYS OVER THERE.

"Well, look who's here," Arachnid says. He lounges on a rumpled hill of blue tarps, which shimmer like water in the lamplight. Rose and Sirloin shuffle through papers, sitting on giant wooden spools and drinking expired cans of Geronimo soda.

Behind them other kids I recognize but have never met take me in with baggy eyes as I cross the warehouse floor. A skinny chick named Torpedo stands, arms folded, draped in a Fillmore Drama Club sweatshirt, her braces fencing back her gnarled teeth. A huge dude I call Kegger, whose fat factor overshadows even his dirty dreadlocks, switches plugs in a computer drive, stacking computer disks into a fortress around him.

A drop of something lands on my head, and I glance up toward the ceiling, where Wicked Witch pours Clear Sweet citrus drink from a bottle. I can smell the burst of lemony flavor. Up there catwalks crisscross the saggy ceiling, leading down to the floor by fire-escape stairs and sliding black ladders. Wicked Witch gives me the finger and walks back across the walkway to the windowsill, where she keeps a lonely lookout. She guards a trio of fat-ass orange extension cords that run out the open window and toward a power line that stands near the warehouse. Digging in her ear, Wicked Witch adjusts the reception on her portable TV antenna and then turns up the volume.

Kerouac whistles me over to an office door that looks strangely out of place in between the men's and women's restrooms. He blows out the candle in his little lantern and then hands it to me so he can flip through a ring of keys on his metal-studded belt. When he finds the right key, he unlocks the office and kicks the door open with a bang.

Against the shelves tilt columns of file boxes stuffed to the flattened lids with paperwork. An enormous wooden desk hogs the center of the room, missing rough chunks like a gnawed bone. Black graffiti bleeds over every inch. Kerouac whips his Indians cap so it lands perfectly on a coatrack in the corner like he's Mr. Smooth, and he sinks into an office chair that barfs stuffing.

"You have to understand something, Arty-man," he says. "The world's pretty tough. You know that better than anybody. It ain't any easier for guys like us. You've got to pick up scraps when you can. I tell everybody who comes to me the same damn thing: You gotta make things happen. 'Cause if you don't care enough to make things happen, then why should I care? You read me?"

He lights a new cigarette with a bowling alley matchbook as Rose's head appears around the doorframe. She knocks gently. He waves her in, taking the ragged red binder she carries out of her hands.

"Is this it?" Kerouac says.

"There's only one, all right," Rose says. The other kids start filing through the doorway behind her, and they pack the cramped office until the last few have to press their faces against the smudgy window. Arachnid rests on the doorframe, working at the trapped food in his teeth with his tongue. I can hear Wicked Witch cycling through classic reruns up in her outpost. I can see her through the huge office window, sitting high on the catwalk, just a gnat in the glow of her blue TV tube.

"What is that?" I say. I point to the red binder. I want to know because the name MOORE is stenciled across the cover in permanent marker.

Kerouac tosses the binder on the desk. "This is Kurt's file," he says. "I got one for pretty much everybody. Even you, my man." He pushes the binder across the gnarled desktop. "Take it."

Only in my daydreams have I ever believed something like this existed. I think of the time Kurt drove over my leg on his moped. The time he took all my sheets, soaked them with a hose, and then put them all back on my bed. The time he threw dipping sauces at me during our tenth birthday party at McDonald's, in front of the few friends that I actually had and who I don't have anymore.

You don't forget things like that. I want that red binder so much, it makes me cold inside. I shiver in my sweatshirt. I feel paralyzed, like Kid with No Legs must feel every shitty day of his life.

A kid behind me, I don't know who, touches my shoulder, and even though it sounds weird, that outstretched hand comforts me—at least enough for me to step forward and take the red binder.

Then Kerouac slips his hand into his trench coat, like he might just pull a gun, and whips out a business card. Smoke pours from his mouth. "You're about to start phase one," he says, and he hands the card to me. It has Rose Purdy's personal phone number printed on it in embossed ink.

"Rose worked real hard on this plan," Kerouac says, "and it's a beauty, designed just for you. She's an artist, Arty-man; so use her as best you can. If you have any questions, you call her. Got it? It's all there in the binder, everything you need."

Before I can thank him, he stands up. It reminds me again of how tall he really is, even compared to the others, even compared to Kurt. All the slouched figures gather around us in a grimy group as Kerouac puts his arm around his girlfriend. She smiles up at him with a smile so clean it seems to make the brownish warehouse light whiter. He presses her closely against him.

"Remember one thing," Kerouac says. The coal at the end of his cigarette brightens, making his eyes gleam in the weak light. "You can't save everybody," he says. "But you can save yourself." The rest of them nod in agreement, and some repeat these words of wisdom back to themselves like a mantra.

The roof creaks in the wind, girders and pipes turning over in their sleep. I think about Kurt waiting for me at home. The times we searched through garbage to make use of all the busted stuff. Those long-time-ago days.

"Welcome to Affront, brother," Kerouac says. And damn it if the dude doesn't hug me.

"This is for you," Rose says, and she flips me a small plastic wrapper. "Good luck, Stumpy. You're gonna need it."

In my hand gleams a tiny metal pin, one of those with a snap-on back. It's a stylized letter *A*. I turn the clear package over and see where someone scratched off the price tag. When I look back up, I realize for the first time: the pins. How everyone here has one. Pinned in Kerouac's hat. Stuck in Rose's bloodstained bandage. Hooked on Arachnid's souvenir Batman utility belt. All of them glint red in the warehouse bulbs.

"That'll be ninety-nine cents," Rose says.

"What for?" I say.

"Dues, all right?" she says.

I dig in my jeans for change. Thank god for the penny parade.

DOSSIER

As soon as I get home, I go straight to the bathroom. My hair smells wet and moldy, smoky, like a gas station bathroom. My shoes leave slimy blue prints on the floor; I make a note to go back and clean everything up as good as new before I hit the sack. I lock the door and turn on the fan to block out the sound.

The red binder blows my mind.

It must hold a hundred pages. It starts with section A, family photos. Many of them I have never seen before and didn't even know existed.

Almost all of the pictures of Dad are mug shots from small-town jails, scattered as far as Florida and as close as West Virginia. I had almost forgotten what the guy even looks like. It would be a lie to say that there isn't a spooky resemblance between him and Kurt.

The snapshots of Grampa were taken when he was older, from the time when I knew him best. I'm in most of these pictures; Kurt, too. The three of us at the store. At the old factory. Grampa fixing a fence for a friend up the street. Where had Kerouac gotten them?

In her pictures Mom's ass is cemented to the seat of her exercise bike, or she's in traffic on the way to the office, chugging coffee behind the dashboard of the Honda. I don't know who took these pictures, but whoever it was used some fancy telephoto lens, 'cause I can practically see every clogged pore on Mom's face.

Section B lists Kurt's interests. It's mostly made up of ads torn from magazines, followed by some written report that gets too psychological to try to make sense of. Kerouac and Rose haven't missed a beat. They include all the big things I remember about Kurt. Lacrosse, Magic Johnson, these complicated board games with cardboard tiles that no one else understood how to play, and David Bowie (but only during the Ziggy Stardust period). They even mention his secret love for stitching, which Grampa first showed him how to do the time Kurt needed to fix a pair of torn church slacks. No one knows about that but me—or so I thought.

When I come to the end of section B, I notice a plastic divider for section C but no material.

As I page back through, I can't help but wonder if those goofy things are still important to him. I don't care all that much, but it makes me realize how long it's been since he and I have actually had a civilized conversation.

It also makes me nervous about what might be in my own secret binder. The first thing that comes to mind is my supposedly secret obsession with Leslie Dermott. That would be bad.

A low creak sounds from the floorboards outside the bathroom.

Then there comes a knock on the door. I shove the binder under a pile of rumpled towels and look in the mirror, fixing my hair for some unknown reason, like I'm answering the door for my prom date or something.

I open the door to find Mom hunched in her bathrobe, her face scrunched up like one of those shrunken heads in old jungle movies. "What gives, Arty?" she says. Her raspy croak sounds like a man's voice. "It's, like, three in the morning."

"Personal stuff," I say. It's the best thing to say to a nosy parent, and it usually works. I pray she doesn't catch the red binder peeking from under the tattered washcloth and the dirty undies.

Luckily, she's about as brain-dead as they come right now. She zones right through me, zombie style. "Good," she says. "Nice to know you're not plotting world domination. That would be bad. Whatever it is, just take care of it and hit the sack, will you? This six hours of sleep is the only time off I get."

"Got it," I say, sending a sweet smile her way.

"You shouldn't waste sleep," she mumbles. "Probably why you're so testy all the time. Sleep is important, like breakfast. You should—"

But she doesn't finish, and swings forward to close the door for me, probably because she is about to fall over and needs something to lean on. As soon as the door clicks shut, I push the lock back in before returning to work. I hardly notice the way my heart has started to gallop heavily inside my chest.

I pull the topmost dirty towels off the pile and find the three-ring binder spread open with its pages hanging by only one of the three rings. The dividers are crumpled in a few places, and some of the photos are wet. For the first time, I notice that there's a large green envelope sticking from the back pocket. I reach inside and slide out a paper-clipped packet bristling with Post-it notes and bathed in highlighter. Scrawled across the front of the green envelope are the words *Phase One*.

Right on top sits an eight-by-ten-inch color photograph of a girl I recognize immediately. She goes to our school, and I often pass her in the hallway on the way to my second-floor advanced algebra class. A professional took the portrait, which brings out her comfortable soft-lipped smile and the shine in her sandy brown hair. On the back is a label that says MARY FIELDER in messy block letters, similar to the style bored kids use to carve their names into desktops. I know that name. A profile follows, a summary of who Mary Fielder is and what she likes—kind of like a smaller version of Kurt's whole notebook but squashed into a paragraph.

Behind the photo a piece of paper flutters, paper-clipped to the glossy plastic sleeve. It's a letter with my name on the top, and checking the signature, I discover that it's from Oil Change herself, Mrs. Affront— Rose Purdy. I read:

(ARTY) SHORT STUFF,

See this chick? She is the object of your ugly brother's desire. Phase one involves a creative writing assignment. We're going to be starting a little pen pal thing, and you have to play the part of Mary Fielder. Fun, huh? You write a letter to your brother and then hand it off to me, and I'll give it that girly OOMPH! Then our handwriting expert, Sergio, will take care of the handwriting thing, all hearts and bubbles—the works. You should be glad we were able to get Sergio on such short notice. He's the best there is.

Big bro will eat these up; trust me. Hook, line, and sinker. Have a little fun with it; be wild—it's up to you, Tiny. Just write me some magic with one of your itty-bitty pens, and when you're done, dump the letter in locker 274. That's our official dead-drop box. I'll take it from there. Even bought some nice flowery, perfumed stationery that fits this chick to a tee.

BTW, tell anyone about this, and you'll wish you'd never laid eyes on me.

R☉S E

The O in her signature is a greasy thumbprint. Real cute.

I can't believe it. The school underground gave me homework.

I set the red binder onto the trash can with the used Q-tips and oily zit pads. Climbing onto my bathroom footstool, I kneel on the bathroom counter, with my forehead against the mirror. The glass is cold and my reflection blurs when I exhale. I can almost feel Kurt breathing through the drywall and the medicine cabinet, the thick rise and fall of his blobby body. I hear his snore, a noise they noted several times in his secret Affront file.

As I listen to him, I start to brainstorm. I can't help myself. When years have passed between yourself and a person, it's not hard to find words you might have said had you not been terrified.

Rose even planned ahead enough to tuck scrap paper and a pen into the back pocket of the binder. The paper is blank on one side but has old typing on the other. At the top of some pages it says: *Affront Minutes—4/15* and *Re: Mr. Zim's after school "study sessions" with female students*. I turn to a blank side, take the top off the pen, and look in the mirror. I seem even shorter than normal, just a fleck of dust with a bad haircut and no balls, barely able to see over the edge of the cluttered counter. I can't look for very long. It makes me tired, and sad, and it makes me think of Grampa when he used to shave in this very same mirror.

I sit down on the closed toilet and begin to write:

Dear Kurt,

    Hi. Do you know who this is? It's Mary Fielder. How are you? I've wanted to write you this letter for a long time, but I've always been a little nervous about it. Do you know the feeling? Do you know what it's like to be scared of something?

THE HALF NAKED
AND THE DEAD

It's Friday morning, and I hold a letter in my hand—
but not one of mine.

Using the doodles and signatures, I piece together
the message's flight path. Apparently Peanut slid it
to Two Tone, the kid who sits next to him in Ms.
Gregorovich's comp class. Two Tone then bounced it
to Yvette and Yolanda in the hall, and they ditched it
to Sausage Gravy at his locker. Hoping it involved sex,
Sausage Gravy gave it a once-over and, disappointed,
crumpled it into a ball and dropped it on the floor
of the science lab. From there Ass-That-Won't-Quit
curled it in her fingers before Mr. Papaparus spotted it.
After that Ass-That-Won't-Quit flicked the note like a
paper football across American studies to the opposite

wall, where I was resting my head on my desk and sulking. That's when I picked it up. The note says:

P,
I heard that ogre freshman Moore
kidnapped Millie. Gonna sell her to
Broomtown High for next
Homecoming.
Can you f'in believe it?
P.S. Gregorovich is such a hor.

There's a knock at the door.

Ms. Wessin ignores the noise at first, gritting her teeth as the knuckles ricochet off the wood. She only has twenty more minutes to go before school is out for the weekend, before she can unwind, probably alone, in front of a fake fireplace, with a five-dollar bottle of wine from the drugstore. But when Wessin can stand the knocking no longer, she slides off her table and opens the door.

The girl I call Funnel Cake appears and snaps a green principal's slip in Wessin's face like it's a speeding ticket. She's got these red pigtails that curl out from the side of her head like a couple of pastries.

Sensing news, the class shuts up. No one breathes until Wessin does, and when she eventually sighs, giggles ripple across the room like the wave at a basketball game. The green principal's slip means only one thing at Fillmore High: Someone is in seriously deep doo-doo.

Wessin strides slowly down the aisles, staring at the green paper slip like it's a big cash tip she's trying to decide what to do with. She stops at Kerouac's desk, the majority of which is occupied with his bald sleeping head. She kicks his desk leg, causing him to snort. I can't imagine what that freak must be dreaming about. Rose Purdy splayed on a car hood dressed only in a welder's mask?

When Kerouac opens his mouth and says, "Give it to me, Ms. Wessin," in his sleep, our classmates lose it. It's impressive, because nothing has been able to make a dent in our attention all period. Any period. Teachers' words bounce off our faces like Ping-Pong balls.

"That's pretty good," Ms. Wessin says, patting Kerouac's head like she's spanking him. "Now get up."

Turning his slick head, my new friend grins at her, totally conscious and totally creepy. He raises his head off the desk and leaves a little smear of sweat on the surface. "Good dreams always gotta end," he says, winking at her.

"You've been summoned," Ms. Wessin says, slapping the green slip down.

"It must be my rich biological father," Kerouac says, kicking back his chair and standing up. "I knew he'd come back for me one day." Wessin doesn't reply but starts back toward the front of the class.

As he heads for the door, Kerouac reads the green slip. When he reaches the end, he suddenly stops in midmosey right by my desk in the back row. He glances at Wessin, who is still making her way to the front, and then looks down at me. "Follow me," he whispers.

"What?"

"Come on," he says. "You have to see this. It's huge."

"I'm not cutting class," I say, but I only half believe it. The kids around me are turning in their seats, whispering now, too, and I want to kill Kerouac for doing this to me.

"It's Millie," he says, spinning toward the door and grabbing the knob. Then, just like magic, he's gone. The classroom door hangs open, squeaking in his wake.

I don't need any more encouragement than "It's Millie." Apparently, neither do the kids in some nearby desks. Backpacks and purses fly. I look up, and four of them are out the door—Night Brace, Sausage Gravy, Snots, and Dirt Lip—then a lone stranger whose duffel bag gets caught on the doorknob. He cusses and wiggles free into the hallway just as Wessin turns.

"What in the heck . . ." she says.

The name "Millie" rockets across class on the lips of the back-row dwellers. Nervous eyes glance at Wessin and then at the door. The teachers can't keep us from knowing what's going on. They made the mistake of thinking we'd lose interest in the Millie thing, thinking we'd go on with business as usual. Fat chance.

Then another kid bolts, a kid in the second row I call Creamed Corn. He trips on his desk leg but regains his balance just in time to bite it on the hallway floor.

"Get back here, Carl!" Wessin runs to the doorway, turning her back on us, but then freezes in the hallway just outside the classroom and does a very dramatic double take. "Good lord."

I can hear it now—the hallway roars with kids.

That's it. Bodies avalanche through the door and collide in the hall, meeting head-on with more frenzied students from other classes. Wessin has barely enough time to step aside so as not to get crushed by the stampede of students in trench coats and tiny T-shirts. Then she's far behind, trying in vain to seduce us back to the sexiness of American studies, the thrill of the cotton gin and labor unions.

Anarchy has gripped Fillmore High. Every class, from mythology to metal shop, has trickled from its classroom and crammed the wide hallways, the name "Millie" dancing over the tops of our heads. Immediately the crowd turns into a stream and gains direction. I get caught up in the buzz and let the current pull me along.

Appearing from what seems like nowhere as I drift by my locker, Leslie practically tackles me, she's so excited. It hits me again, how pretty she is in person—the face of an angel on the body of a rock-climbing supermodel.

"Arty!" she says, flapping her hands in a blur. "It's Code Green, Code Green."

"What's 'Code Green'?" I say. I don't bother to ask her why she wasn't in class. Beautiful people have their reasons.

"I have no idea," she says, "but that's what I heard some kids calling it. Isn't it amazing? There was something on those little slips, though, the ones that were supposedly from the principal. Kids in a bunch of classrooms got one, and now they're all leaving."

"Who's leaving?" I say.

"Everybody," she says, throwing her arms out into the moving swarm. "I heard that some people are getting into their cars and everything. I don't know where they're going, but someone does." Her eyebrows sharpen into an evil point above her nose. "I think we should follow them."

This is the kind of situation in which I need to step up and be decisive, manly. So I stick my neck out like a confident person, which I'm not, and I nod like I know what I'm doing, which I don't. "Let's go."

My reward is that Leslie does this thing with my

hair, where she kind of ruffles the back and yanks a few stray strands just hard enough to hurt. Tingles blast up my spine like a string of firecrackers. I never thought any girl would touch me on purpose like that.

It looks like Leslie wasn't the only one to hear about Code Green. Half the student body pours through the back doors, kids scurrying for transportation, trying to get into their cars before the leaders take off. Some of the kids smell drunk already. Every few seconds some confused teachers exit the building, see the chaos, and open their mouths to shout orders.

But who would they shout at? There are hundreds of us, and we will not be told what to do today.

I notice Kurt under a tree, resting on the seat of his Yamaha. He watches the activity deadpan, a textbook open on the black seat-cushion in front of him. As the lot empties, his hands stay in his pockets like they're fused to his thighs. Some girls flash him from a Jeep, but even they don't get a reaction. He doesn't even smile. This craziness was the sort of thing he lived for back in his delinquent days, after Dad left. And just because he hasn't gotten picked up by the cops recently doesn't mean he's gone and turned saint or anything.

Cars clog the parking lot exits. Leslie leads me to her white Jetta and pops the auto locks with her key chain. She sings a duet with the car stereo as we wait our turn. Exhaust blankets the rest of the world in a smoke screen, and the heat makes the black road shimmer. Leslie seems very *there,* alive, though she never quite gets the words to the song right. I love every second of it. Every sing-along beat. This must be what it's like to know who you are, and to enjoy it.

We follow the flow of traffic as it winds through side streets and intersections. A squad of teachers try to keep up in their cheap imports and station wagons with baby seats. They finally seize the upper hand at the long stoplight at Ninth-Green Street, where Ms. Wessin and Mr. Glean run the red light in same-model-but-different-year Hondas and cut our student convoy in two. The two of them idle as the rest of the faculty pull in behind them one at a time, before continuing on after the green-slip holders, the mysterious chosen ones.

Those of us in the second group now have to deal with the teachers. As we drive, Mrs. Hirschman and Coach Plack lean from the back of a blue Chevy Suburban and try to shoo us kids away, mouthing, "Go home," over and over. Like that's going to happen. We trail them all the way through town to Center Junction, east onto Old Quarry Road, and then over the railroad tracks to the entrance of the old sandstone quarry.

Last in the faculty line, Mr. Forke executes a fancy spinout in his aqua blue Saturn and tries to block the gate to the old mining site. But it's too little too late. Vaseline leads the way, wobbling around the rubble and up the ridge in his Navigator, then down to the other side, where the road picks up. Mr. Forke shakes his fist maniacally and curses Vaseline, but some punk in the back of a Jeep farts through a portable megaphone and drowns him out.

Leslie's Jetta manages the off-road excursion easily, and soon we shoot down the gravel road, pebbles clacking off the windshield from the convertible ahead of us. The walls of the quarry loom on either side, huge and red, scarred from dynamite and littered with burned-out machinery. I listen to the roar of engines ring off the canyons.

Cars start to pull over when the drivers see the circle of police cruisers up ahead. Cops mill around with hands on their hips and hat brims pulled down low. They draw plans in the dust with twigs. Our teachers sit parked with engines running, like they're about to start a drag race. I don't understand what they're waiting for, all those wrinkled faces pressed against air-conditioned windows.

Then Leslie gasps and hits the brakes. "Arty, look," she says.

I follow her gaze, starting up from the quarry floor to the wall and then to the cliff. And I see what all the fuss is about.

Millie the Turtle sways from a rusted crane with a noose of cable around her stone neck. The crane's great steel arm creaks with her weight, and I don't know how it stays up there, as fossilized as it is, protruding from the cliffs, a hundred feet from the ground.

Leslie and I get out and join the growing mob by the police prowlers. Most of the kids absorb the moment quietly with jaw-dropped astonishment. Others argue conspiracy theories and trade cigarettes. We push our way through the pot smoke to the front to get a better look.

"They lynched Millie," Gus Van Mussberger says from behind me. Gus remains the one guy in school who I didn't give a goofy name to—apart from Leslie, that is. I don't remember why, exactly, but I'm sure it has something to do with how ridiculous he is even without a nickname. He licks his goatee, which he does when he thinks really hard. A giant joint smokes in his fingers.

"Bitches," someone on my right says.

"What the hell's she got on?" Gus says.

"Dude, it's a bra, totally," the kid on my right says.

"I think he's right," Leslie says.

Gus checks Leslie out with swooping eyes. Then he looks at me and scrunches his forehead, like he's trying to solve some complex algebra problem.

"Shit, man," the kid on my right says. "That's not just some bra. You know what that is?"

"What? What is it?" I say. I can't see anything. I stretch my neck to find cracks in the crowd as people shove closer, but I can only make out the steel cable and a bunch of pimply shoulders.

"It's a plus-size," a girl says. "A *mega*-plus." She sweeps her blond bob from her face. "I thought those were illegal."

"I feel like I'm on *X* right now," Gus Van Mussberger says under his breath.

Leslie turns and catches me balancing on my toes. "Here," she says, and hunches down, motioning for me to climb onto her back.

I hesitate. I should be used to people doing this kind of thing by now, but I'm not. Sometimes I still have dreams about looking down on people. It's that hard to get over.

I don't realize Leslie's being serious until I catch her fantastic grin. She clucks and drops her shoulders. "Going up," she says.

Rather than fighting her, I climb on. Her moisturized skin feels baby-doll smooth, and she's surprisingly sturdy for a chick. I smell her perfume radiating from the part in her hair and immediately recognize it as Octane. Mom rips the free samples from fashion magazines and leaves them in the kitchen trash can.

Gus gawks at the two of us. Others do, too. Pinochle, Cosby Sweaters, Binge-and-Purge, Olga, Camel Toe, and Fire Engine. Why am I up here? I've spent a whole year staying out of people's way in the shadows. Yet here I am riding Leslie Dermott's back like some goblin horse-jockey.

I don't get down. I convince myself that I can't. I squeeze my fingers together and lock my knuckles. I won't go, because this may be the only time I get to smell that perfume on a person and not from a trash can. This may be the only time I hold Leslie, even though she's really holding me. I feel safe up here, like no one can touch me.

A deep twanging vibrates through the quarry, and all eyes snap back up to the turtle. The cable, the noose, it's breaking.

The police spring from their cars and hurriedly herd people back. Leslie shudders, and I feel our breathing synchronize. Then the wire makes an awful pinging noise like a massive guitar string snapping, and it splits apart into shreds.

Millie's fall fills the vacuum of those few, and supernaturally silent, seconds when no one can find the breath to say anything.

Her mammoth feet hit first and detonate. Everyone leaps backward in a group to avoid the incoming shrapnel as Millie disintegrates from the bottom up in a blooming cloud of dust. The ground shakes. It must be just like the old mining days again, dynamite sticks and a typhoon of earth, rubble, and grit. A rolling wave of debris sweeps over the spectators, and I cover my eyes, burying my face in the back of Leslie's shirt.

When I look up, Millie is gone. My favorite smack-talking boxing turtle has been reduced to a heap of chunks. With her lower half vaporized, her upper half collapses in several enormous sections that fall away like slices of an orange. Then only her head remains. It rolls off one muscled turtle shoulder and plops heavily to the dirt. It sits there in the middle of the mess, making Millie look like a kid buried up to his neck at the beach.

"Holy shit," Gus Van Mussberger says, his teeth now crunchy with grime.

"Yeah," the blond with the bob says.

A hush falls over the canyon, and no one speaks for a good minute, maybe out of respect or something. Eventually the teachers order us to go home. Delinquents linger and try skimming the police line to snag bits of Millie. The cops do their best, but even they can't catch the kid with the megaphone. He takes off his shirt and runs in figure eights around the yellow tape, whooping like Crazy Horse. He farts into the megaphone again.

Leslie carries me back to the Jetta on her shoulders.

That's when it happens, the funniest thing.

As we pass through the herd, a tall guy with a baseball hat and glasses raises his hand and shouts, "Yo! Arty, give it up, man!" Leslie changes course, and I smack Tall Guy's palm. To our left, a voice calls out, "Come on, man, give me some of that!" And before I know it, I'm surveying an ocean of tanned hands and faces. I hit them all, smacking each palm like it's the first, saying dumb crap I don't even remember, and the entire time Leslie laughs and whirls me around, fetching comments of her own and making sure I share the love.

With my arms around her neck, I can feel the interlocking joints of Leslie's collarbone. I can smell that smack-in-the-face scent of Octane in her soft hair, and taste the dust that is Millie grating in my mouth and lodged between my teeth. From up here I can see the tips of Southworth's two biggest buildings glittering in the afternoon light. Life is perfect. Tall.

At eye level Gus Van Mussberger shakes his gigantic head and scratches his goatee. "Dude, who the hell are you?"

And I know just what to tell him.

"I'm Arty Moore."

AGAINST THE ROPES

 THE SCHOOL NEWSLETTER OF

THE FILLMORE HIGH SCHOOL BOXING TURTLES

"A turtle only makes progress when it sticks out its neck."
—Anonymous

WEEK OF MAY 23–29

🐢 Don't forget the schoolwide "Casino Night Party" (theme as of yet undetermined) on June 3rd. Make memories that will last a lifetime! Try things you've never tried before! Drink punch!

🐢 Stay alert! If you have any information about what happened to our beloved Millie the Boxing Turtle, please report it to a teacher or Principal Malone. Telling on a person doesn't make you a rat!

🐢 WORK AT SOUTHWORTH MALL—Who needs school? Working is where it's at! Call 555-CASH.

🐢 Services: I can detail cars with the best of them. Need a new paint job? Wheel alignment steering you in the wrong direction? Don't trust the guys; call me: Rose Purdy @ 457-7022.

🐢 **NEW:** Astronomy Club, Friday nights at 11:00 in the field across from Radar Run. Bring a telescope, a blanket, and a close friend. Call Leslie: 579-9877.

MEAT LOCKER

"Two weeks?" she says. "Is that all? It feels like years, I swear."

"Two weeks exactly as of yesterday," I say. "That's when we met."

"Then we need to celebrate our anniversary," Leslie says, and she claps her hands.

It's a Wednesday afternoon, not exactly the choice time for a big anniversary party. And I don't feel like celebrating. I gaze out onto the lawn where Camilla wrestles with a hose like it's some kind of angry alien tentacle. I want to slide the glass door open and walk out to help her, but I'm afraid of what Leslie might say if I do. Camilla falls over into a hedge and disappears. The bushes shake.

It seems like the longest two weeks of all time. Two weeks with the girl I've always wanted, or thought I wanted. Two weeks of hiding in my room, of dropping off letters, of spending time with Leslie—and of keeping my distance from my own twin brother. Two weeks, and what do I have to show for it?

The new Kurt is what I have to show for it.

The guy seems almost happy, if that was ever possible. He clomps all over the house with a smile on his big fat face, and he hasn't laid a hand on me since the day he found that first envelope waiting for him in his locker. I've written five letters since then. Each one grows more detailed and intimate. I've created a masterpiece in this fictional Mary Fielder, and I almost wish I knew more about the real girl, because every time I write in her voice, I feel closer to her.

Rose counted on Kurt to be too chicken to actually talk to Mary Fielder. It was a key part of her plan. The few times he actually shows his face in the school hallway, I catch him sending a smile Mary's way, vibes of emotion that practically ripple like heat waves. I'm amazed no one's picked up on them yet. No one, that is, but Mary. She registers every last glance, and squirms when she sees him come up over the stairs and at her like a tidal wave.

Poor idiot Kurt is so convinced by the girlie loops and curves of the letters' pink script, that he'd probably ask Mary out on a date before he even spoke to her in person. Little does he know that her every word is straight from my mind—with a little help from the talented hand of Sergio, Rose Purdy's master forger.

The Dermotts love earth tones. That much I'm sure of. Everything in their house on Pinewood Terrace, from the sectional couch to the ceramic liquid-soap dispenser in the bathroom, smacks of money and a lack of personality. The huge kitchen opens up into an equally enormous bar and rec room that looks like a floor display in a furniture store—sterile, perfectly arranged and decorated. A room that draws every shopper's eye, but a place in which no human being would ever actually want to hang out. I've spent a lot of time around here these last two weeks, and I'm pretty sure I've read every magazine on the cut-glass-and-marble coffee table twice, even *Pastry Art & Design*.

Leslie stands behind the kitchen-counter island and rolls a massive amoeba of dough out in front of her on a sheet of waxed paper. She wears a Sorbonne T-shirt that's so thin from washing that it's painfully obvious she's not wearing a bra. That's half the reason I'm staring my hardest out the window. The other half is that I know she's wearing that shirt on purpose, that she wants me to look. This makes me worry about what we're doing here together in the first place.

I'd rather watch Camilla wriggle around on her back and stab the hose with hedge trimmers. Now *that's* entertainment.

"Who are these for again?" I say. "The Astronomy Club?" The baking hasn't been going well. Her shirt swims in batter.

"The cast of *Merry Wives of Windsor*, silly," she says, stirring a bowl of glaze. "Morning rehearsal starts this week. Let's see. That means I get out of my first two periods for the rest of the year. Then we only have a month until opening night. The school's first 'Shakespeare on a Football Field' theater festival. I know it's technically only a couple of more weeks till school's out, but two periods of freedom is better than nothing."

"Sounds good to me," I say. I'm impressed. She's discovered a useful reason to be in a school play.

"I don't talk about the show too much, do I?" she says. But before I can gauge her expression, she ducks below the counter. No doubt she's fiddling with the deep fryer she bought specifically for Shakespeare doughnut making.

"What show?" I say. It's supposed to be funny, in a bitter, hinting kind of way.

The answer is yes. Yes, she talks about the show all the time, ever since she started rehearsals. Theater dominates between her talk of forming a Future Caterers Club and her momentary obsession with restrictive colon-cleansing diets. She makes ER doctors look like couch potatoes.

"I told you about Vincent, right?" she says. "He's amazing."

"Who?" I know exactly the guy she's talking about.

"Vincent Nguyen."

"Sure, Vincent." I say. Sure, Vincent. Tall, Tibetan or something, showed up in Southworth halfway through Christmas break, wears a lot of denim shirts and khakis. I heard he swims like some kind of crazy genius fish. Sure, Vincent. "What about him?"

"He's the lead in the show. He's remarkable." She raises her hands over her head to emphasize Vincent's awe-inspiring power. "I mean, he's really shy during the breaks, but when we get going, he practically blows the roof off the place every time. What a voice. You'd like him, Arty."

"You bet," I say. Then something occurs to me. "This is a Shakespeare musical?"

"Of course," she says, forming a plump ring of dough with her fingers. "I adapted it. I'm also the first female Falstaff in the history of Millard Fillmore High School."

"Big surprise," I say. She misses the sarcasm.

"You know," she says, "according to rumor, Vincent tried to hang himself before he moved here.

Suicide, Arty. Isn't that the worst thing you've ever heard? Well, isn't it?" She walks from behind the counter to a spot about a foot from my face, and she stands with her hands on her hips, flung batter across her nose like war paint.

"Sure," I say, with about as much enthusiasm as a guy in a coma.

"That's one of the reasons I like you so much, Arty," she says. "You really understand what it's like to have a hard time. I respect that. The rest of us can learn a lot from guys like you."

I wish I had the right comeback balanced on the tip of my tongue. Because then no matter how good she looks filling that shirt, I'd tell her how I really feel. How I'm sick of customers at the store asking me if I'm a lost little boy. That I don't want to teach anyone anything.

But before I can come up with something, she raises a drippy finger and offers it to me. Sweet doughnut gunk hangs in stalactites from her painted nail. "Have some," she says. "Give a try."

It's easy to lose track when a girl in low-hanging cotton offers you pure sugar from her fingertip. She laughs. And I'm that dumb bastard in American studies class all over again, nuts for the girl with the perfect face and the body, fooled by all the camera tricks and pyrotechnics.

As I gag on Leslie's knuckle, I hear a cough from the hallway. One of those "I'm right here, so get a room" coughs.

Camilla comes in lugging a bright red vacuum cleaner and showing off new blond streaks. Grass stains scar her frilly apron. She blows a bubble of green gum and fires up the Dirt Devil.

The phone rings, and Leslie takes it into a back room so she can hear better. I stand to one side as Camilla cleans around the coffee table and the bookshelves. After vacuuming she walks over to the stereo, which takes up the whole freaking wall like we're in the Batcave or something, and she puts in this CD.

Now, I don't know what the two guys are saying 'cause it's in Spanish, but they both seem pretty happy as they sing. It sounds like maybe they're smiling as they belt it out, and maybe they're looking back and forth at each other and trying not to bust out laughing from some inside joke they've shared since they were kids.

Camilla dusts the African urns on the shelf above the bar, which I've seen her dust every afternoon. She picks up Leslie's discarded sweatshirts and folds them up nicely, stacking them on a kitchen stool. From her holster of cleansers, she whips out a bottle of hair volumizer and fluffs the hair on the life-size replica of Chewbacca from *Star Wars*. Then she takes a step back to inspect her work, and a smile crosses her delicate face. She starts on the island in the kitchen, putting dishes in the sink, rinsing them carefully, and then arranging them in the dishwasher before turning it on. Her black-and-blond hair swishes around in its braid as she scours the slime-encrusted stovetop and hums along to the music.

I like watching her clean up, making Leslie's mess just a memory. She scrubs at streaks on the counter with one hand and Windexes the windows over the sink with the other. Afterward she replaces the browning flowers in the vase with fresh ones from a wicker basket.

For that couple of minutes, I feel great, the best I've felt in as long as I can remember. Those two happy Mexican dudes croon and strum their guitars, and Camilla moves like she's dancing in streams of liquid Comet.

As she runs the disposal and wipes dust balls from her apron, she looks up at me and nods. A smile. She leaves the kitchen, only to return for the vacuum, which she straps across her back. Attachments and hoses dangle over and around her shoulders as she marches down the hall of mirrors that leads to the inner atrium. She looks like some kind of paratrooper, and I listen to her scuff down the hallway, her tiny feet squeaking on the polished marble.

She must have taken that great CD with her, because when I go to play the song with those two singing nuts again, the disk tray is empty. The tune still rings in my head, though, and it's difficult not to feel better about life, and Leslie, and the stupid plan and all its silly pieces. If only Kerouac and Rose could hear those Spanish guys crowing. They'd probably lighten up.

That's what I need to do, relax. I need to remember that any guy in school would gladly switch positions with me in a heartbeat. And Leslie, though weird, is a nice person overall, a go-getter, a real Eleanor Roosevelt type, just hotter.

I wait for Leslie and poke around the bar in the living room. The gigantic walk-in stainless-steel fridge has this showy St. Pauli Girl beer light swinging from it, a blond model plastered over the front, and it's totally freaky, because if you squint just enough, that St. Pauli Girl could totally be a blond Leslie.

There's nothing in the fridge of interest, only lines of unopened vodka bottles with gold-rimmed caps and red-fringed stickers, tucked together like a line of snazzy soldiers.

Then I see something I never noticed before. A gray curtain hangs from a wooden rod on the back wall of the room by the old cigar-store Indian. I push the flowing fabric out of the way, and there, complete with a porthole, stands another metal door, one that resembles the fridge door except that this one has a tiny wheel where the handle's supposed to be. I touch the surface and it's cool, and the glass on the small, circular window smudges with moisture. It's like I'm standing outside a docked submarine or something. At the top of the door is bolted a sign that reads OUTGOING in yellow stencil.

I check to see if anyone else is in the room, and then take the heavy silver wheel and twist, leaving a palm print that shrinks up and vanishes in a matter of seconds. The seal breaks wind like I'm invading a tomb that's been hidden for centuries. A nasty stench hits me hard across the face: formaldehyde, or maybe pure alcohol; something sickeningly sour.

I can see my breath as it rises up to blend with tufts of thick mist that tumble from blowers on the ceiling. Metal racks hold miniature body bags all the way back to the far wall. Almost everything I can think of that can be dissected is sealed in cloudy packets on the iced silver rungs: dogs, pigs, cats, frogs, goats, fish, mice, and squid. One low platform supports nothing but a messy collection of small bags labeled *Eyeballs*.

A chill runs through my body just as Leslie pinches my shoulder. I clutch my chest and shoot Leslie a glare.

"You found Dad's stash," she says.

"A mad scientist's lab," I say. Her perfume smells stale, and my immediate reaction is to pull away.

"You wish," she says, and leads me back out of the fridge. "No evil genius, just a dealer of delectable dissectibles. He likes to drink after he works. Mix business with pleasure." She shuts the door, and the air around the bar seems to gasp. The crisp stench of body bags lingers, settling on the Chex Mix on the counter.

"The phone's for you," she says, handing it over.

"For me?"

"Yeah, someone beeped in when I was finishing up with Vincent."

Vincent? And who's calling for me here, anyway? I put the receiver to my ear and hear unmistakable heavy breathing.

"Hello," I say.

"You know who this is," a husky voice says. I can just imagine Rose Purdy on the other end, riveting something, practicing her power sanding.

"Yes," I say.

"It's time to finish up phase one," she says. "Do you have what it takes to play hardball?" Then the line goes dead. My throat dries up, and I keep the phone against my ear for a long time.

When we leave the house, I can still smell frozen pigs on my clothes, even in the heat of the afternoon sun. I stink like a cow eyeball all the way across the driveway.

Camilla performs athletic stretches in the topiary garden. When she finishes she mows the lawn, in a sports bra and sandals.

Right now she's my favorite person in the whole world.

STRiP MĀLL

I dream of Millie and Kurt frozen solid and stacked on long metal rows, like the insides of a grocery store freezer, or Mr. Dermott's secret room behind the St. Pauli Girl light.

In my nightmare, someone I bet is Mr. Dermott orders whole rooms of frozen animals for dissecting, truck after truck of them, and they arrive one truckload after another all night long. He keeps saying over and over, "Where are the turtles? Where are the turtles?" And then at the very end of the night, just before sunrise, this special truck pulls up, kind of like a bread delivery truck, and this small dude in a white suit hops out with a clipboard, and Mr. Dermott has to sign some paperwork on the dotted line. When Mr. Dermott's done, the small dude wheels out Millie and Kurt crammed together on this rattling dolly cart, their very different faces frozen in frosty smiles.

But then a weird thing happens. The sun jets up from behind the trees really fast, scary fast, and the small dude in white, he totally freaks, and he cries out and throws an arm up in front of his face. This causes the cart to swerve to one side and then—POW! It jerks and tosses Millie spiraling through the air toward the ground. She shatters into a million mirrorlike pieces on the driveway.

As her pieces fly, the sun makes the asphalt steam, and Kurt, who was frozen, starts to drip.

Suddenly I'm standing there with everyone. And I can't move. And Mr. Dermott and the little white-suited guy just gawk all over the busted Millie chips. They don't notice Kurt, no matter how much I shout at them.

And Kurt thaws and thaws. The ice melts quickly in the hot sun and morning-traffic exhaust, and I see him about to break from his shell. Soon his face moves, tensing. And he's looking at me. And glaring. And I can't move a muscle.

When I finally snap awake, my sheets are sort of stuck to me, dark with sweat like I was the one who was melting.

I feel to make sure all my parts are there and functioning. Check, check, check. I'm all in one piece, but my hair still stinks like chilled pig stomachs and spread-eagle frogs. So I head for the shower, just in time to hear Kurt bang out through the front door downstairs.

At breakfast Mom says nothing over her cereal. She eyes Kurt's breakfast carnage—a charred frying pan, eggshells, and a flattened cigarette butt—and doesn't touch her food.

It's hard to believe that someone like Mom might have been as good-looking as Leslie when she was young. Well, maybe not that hot, but not what she is now. Mom wears a pair of ratty old sweats and a blue headband that's got a bloodstain on it. Behind her ear is a cigarette, like it's there in case of an emergency, like an insulin shot or something. Without makeup she just looks brittle and chalky white—old. I love her, but she's not what you want to look at over breakfast.

It makes me think of how good Leslie will look at her Astronomy Club meeting tomorrow night, lying back on a blanket with her hair everywhere. She plans to wear an old NASA jumpsuit that she bought online from some ex-pilot—if it's delivered on time. We'll kick back under the stars, and she'll tell me the stories of some constellations, and then she'll make them romantic by applying the stories to the two of us. It's wishful thinking, but it works in helping me forget about my nightmare and eat my stale cereal.

It also reminds me that I have to pick up my telescope.

"Mom, can you drive me to school?" I say.

"I thought you liked to walk," she says, looking up. I'd snapped her out of a thought.

"I need to pick up something from Hobby Hut."

She eyes me carefully. "What?"

"It's a telescope for the school Astronomy Club," I say. "A guy at the hobby store is holding it for me." The store ran out of stock in one week after tons of guys from school read that Leslie is leading the Astronomy Club. Hobby Hut was not prepared for the likes of a telescope feeding frenzy.

"School's almost over," Mom says. "Why are you joining clubs?"

"My friend Leslie is running it," I say. I don't know why she's asking so many questions. What next, one of those interrogation lamps?

"Leslie who drives?" Mom says.

"Yes."

"Where did you get extra money for a telescope?"

"It's a cheap one, and Leslie paid for it."

Mom blinks at this, like a flinch, as if I smacked her across the face. "Oh," she says. "Well, it's good to know we've got some extra money coming in. Next time she wants to buy you something, tell her you need a new sump pump."

"Come on, Mom," I say.

Sighing, she gets up and puts the milk and cereal away, then wipes the kitchen table with a wet paper towel. She tousles my hair. "Is Hobby Hut even open this early?"

"They open at seven," I say.

"Anyone who has a hobby that early needs to see a shrink," she says, plucking the keys off the counter and heading for the stairs. "I'll be down in a second. Get your crap together."

A minute later, Mom comes back down to the kitchen wearing sunglasses, her head wrapped in a red scarf. She looks like some sort of frumpy spy as she leads me across the lawn to the car. My cereal squirms in my stomach as I watch her light a cigarette. It's not even eight o'clock yet, and Mom never smokes before nine. Ever.

In the car she disengages the passenger air bag with the touch of a button. Air bags can kill me. One more disadvantage to being a sideshow shrimp.

Mom fires up a second Winston as she blows by every other car on the road. She drives like she rides exercise bikes. She trims every corner, and she doesn't even slow for the yellow lights when they blink on the brink of red. She turns on the morning radio talk show but then quickly changes the station when an announcer launches into a news update about the Millie the Turtle mystery. Mom finds a classical music station and lets the digital dial sit.

The sun flickers in tree branches, and I close my eyes and inhale the wind from the open window. It smells like pancakes. I think about Leslie and all her exaggerated curves, trying to push my nightmare out of my mind. Leslie. She was almost too perfect. I remember when I first saw her in public—she was *so* nice. During all those months I spent ogling her, I never really imagined what she'd be like in real life. I guess that's the advantage of never talking to a person. You're never disappointed.

I feel Mom pull off the road and slow down. "Come back to us, Your Majesty," she says, pinching my stomach. "Arise." I sit up, opening my eyes, and see Mom corkscrewing her cigarette into the overflowing dashboard ashtray.

The car floats in a dusty ocean of empty parking spaces at the North Southworth Plaza strip mall. The mall's only shops are a mom-and-pop hardware store, a video rental place with outdated posters in the windows, a condemned pet store with a laundry machine on the sidewalk out front, and the depressing end unit that Hobby Hut calls home. A blue hatchback rusts by an overflowing Dumpster, BEST PRICE scrawled on the windshield with soap. Two bearded drifters smoke in a small alley. I bet they're wondering whether our severed limbs would fit into their lumpy duffel bags.

"Wow," I say. "It looks different." It does, a lot different. Last time I was at the Hobby Hut, I was probably seven, buying a Rommel figurine to go with my Afrika Korps WWII miniatures set.

Mom turns the keys, and the car shudders and dies. From behind the dark glasses her eyes look like targets with the bull's-eyes shot out. It gives me the willies. "What are you waiting for?" she says. "Scoot."

So I jump from the car and hightail it into Hobby Hut, the window of which burns brightly with an orange OPEN sign.

Behind the counter stands a guy who can't be much older than I am. His oily hair is parted down the middle in the never-popular "butt crack" style. I can't tell if he's trying to grow a mustache or not, but a small wisp of hair shadows his upper lip. "Can I help you?" he says.

I tell him my name, and he goes into the back closet to root around for my telescope. When he comes back, he holds a rectangular box with a receipt taped to it. "You won't see anything with this," he says. "It's crap." His shirt shows a picture of the Milky Way with a line leading out from it to the words *You Are Here*.

"It doesn't matter," I say, taking the box and turning.

"Leslie Dermott?" the guy says.

I don't know what to say, but end up mumbling, "Uh, yeah."

"Astronomy posers," the guy says, shaking his head. He goes back to gluing tiny trees to a flat piece of plywood covered in fake grass. I'm probably the only customer he'll have all day, which is probably how he wants it.

I go back outside, steering very clear of the bearded drifters in their alley, and climb back into the passenger's seat. Mom smiles at me and says, "Everything go okay, Galileo?" I nod, smiling—so far, so good.

Then I notice that the car keys sit in Mom's lap when they should be dangling from the ignition. The windows are rolled up even though she's working that cigarette like it's the last one on Earth. *So far, so good* just became *to hell in a handbasket.*

"You know, I've been thinking," Mom says. "We don't really communicate. We talk, but what do we really say to each other?" It's parentspeak for a talk about one of the following: sex, drugs, or Mom and Dad are getting a divorce.

"Mom," I say, whining more than I mean to, "I'm going to be late for school."

Then she's Mom again, real Mom, legal assistant, always worried, hard-as-nails Mom. "Cut the act, Arty," she says. "You've been hiding something from me. You and Kurt both. I know it. You're going to tell me what's going on."

"Sir, yes, sir," I say. "I'll turn my life around. Honest. Just don't send me back to juvie."

"Arty, I'm serious," she says, unamused. "Pull it together."

"Fine."

"Listen. You know that I do what I can to help you boys. To help Kurt turn out right, maybe straighten up," she says. Then she looks over her shoulder like she's afraid someone might be listening. "You probably already know this, but your brother has a criminal record. Granted, it's short, but he's got one. Hell, I've seen it, Arty. You think it's cool to have a record at fourteen?"

I never considered for a second that Kurt *didn't* have a criminal record. Dad had a record, and a pretty long one, too. It's only fitting for Kurt to follow in Dad's footsteps. Maybe they could hold a little contest to see who can be the bigger screwup.

"Well?" Mom says.

"No, of course it's not cool," I say.

"So, are you going to tell me what you know?" she says.

"What do I know?" I'm not even sure what she's getting at.

"Did Kurt do it?" she says.

"Do what?" I say. "If you're charging him with

being an asshole, then yes, guilty as charged, Your Honor."

"Quit it," she says. She slumps her shoulders then starts winding a curl of hair that peeks from the side of her scarf. In a second she'll go for another cigarette. "Well, for starters, did he steal that statue? And don't feed me one of your BS stories, Arty. I want truth, hard fact, got it?"

"Steal Millie?" I can't help it. I belt out a huge I-could-really-use-a-good-laugh kind of laugh.

"It's hardly worth gagging over," Mom says. "This is pretty serious. Kurt's been MIA ever since he started high school, and he's done some really stupid crap. I just pray he didn't smash that goofy statue. I know it's not murder, but for god's sake—it's a statue of a turtle. It's the stupidity of the thing that pisses me off. He was doing so much better."

"Doing better at what?" I say. "Chewing his food? Tying his own shoes?"

Mom looks at me, her mouth open with purpose to tell me something, but then she hesitates. "Your brother has had a hard time," she says, and I know it's not what she wanted to say. "You should ease up on him a bit, give him a break."

"'Give him a break'?" I say. I can't believe this.

"Yes," she says. "Just lay off of him every once in a while, will you? You can be a real jerk, Arty."

I want to tell her about all the things Kurt has done

to me over the years. For a long time, I was afraid of what he'd do to me if I told, but not anymore. The problem is, if I tell her now, my whole grand plan goes straight down the toilet. "Kurt's nothing but a screw-up," I say. "He's a loser. That's all."

"That's not all," she says. "He may be a screwup, but he's also your brother."

"So what?" I say, grinding my teeth and staring at the window. I feel as empty as this parking lot. "Dad's my dad, but that doesn't mean anything."

They are the true words of a superjerk, just like Mom said. But I'm too angry to take them back, or care that I've let them out in the first place.

Mom doesn't move for a few seconds. She must be letting the mention of Dad dissipate and vanish like smoke, as if it and he were never there. "I don't know," she says, turning away in frustration, her voice soft. "I can't keep track of either of you guys anymore."

"Mom, Kurt didn't do it," I say, and I believe every word. "It's not possible." I want her to feel okay again.

"I know, I know," she says. "I'm so paranoid. I can't decide what to think."

"Seriously, Mom," I say. "Kurt and what army?"

But I stop talking when I see her finish her Winston and go for another. There's none left in the pack, so she starts picking through the stubs in the ashtray to find one with some tobacco left in it. The sight nauseates me.

Dad did this to her. When he swiped her purse years ago, like she was just some random lady on the street. He made a fool out of her. It was so bad that she had to move, leave town, and start over. I watch her fling some dimes onto the car floor and mutter like a crazy bum, digging in the ashes. She gets this way whenever she thinks about him.

I never should have opened my big mouth.

When she finds nothing to smoke, Mom sighs and clears her throat. "So this is the telescope?" she says, taking the box from my hands. Her voice comes out shaky though she tries hard to sound perfectly normal.

"Yeah," I say.

She takes it, opens the box top, and then slides the black plastic tube out into her palm. Fixing it up against one eye, she gazes out into the parking lot like a pirate looking for a speck of land in the distance.

"The guy says you can't really see anything with it, anyway," I say.

"Then what's the point?" Mom says flatly, handing the telescope back to me.

I don't know what to say.

"Now let's get you to school," she says, flashing a phony smile. "You don't want to be late, do you?" She twists the keys in the ignition and brings the car roaring back to life.

SPLIT

Hands down, this is the best bowl of runny ice cream I've ever eaten. A spilt stream of fudge flows by, down the car hood where we sit and over the front grille. Leslie swirls her finger in it and then writes her name in sugary swirls: *Leslie Anne Dermott*.

The first official meeting of the Fillmore High School Astronony Club is over, and now the stars are ours, Leslie's and mine. The Jetta purrs, its parking lights dimmed, sunken in a dip of the field. We recline under the shade of the five huge radar dishes that scoop up from the tall grass like bionic mushrooms. They tilt, listening as I suck down my hot fudge. I bury my head in Leslie's folded sweatshirt and bang a plastic spoon against my teeth. The crickets in the tall weeds snap, crackle, and pop, and Leslie leans into the car window and taps up the stereo volume to drown out the sound. Across the field a semicircle of parked cars hide under the overhanging trees, and I can only imagine the sounds that those stereos have to drown out.

Is that why I suggested Viking Ice Cream again, because I hope to get lucky, too? What a joke. Making out with me would probably be like making out with someone's little brother.

But I feel free tonight, free to kick back for just a little while, to forget that I'm afraid of the dark and just kind of enjoy the night. Enjoy things like the stars and the dull moon, or sucking on a pink plastic spoon until every last molecule of ice cream is gone.

I can relax because this morning I delivered my last letter as Mary Fielder—and that last letter had a big surprise that not even Kurt saw coming.

Phase one is finished.

I followed Rose's instructions exactly, but I decided to add some flourishes of my own this time. Mary, my version, has decided that she can't write to Kurt anymore. See, she asked all her friends about him, and everything she heard back was bad.

The stories made her sick. Like the time he killed that cat with a two-by-four outside the Baptist church, a rumor I just thought up one morning in the shower. And it made her blush with shame, but also with anger, when she heard about how he moonlights in booths at the adult video store on Pine Street. For all

I know he's only done that once, but once was enough for me to make up the rest and still have it carry some weight.

It came to the point that I was having too many good ideas, like a creative overload, and I had to stop or go crazy. I never knew I was so good at telling stories, even if they are loads of crap. I must have some need to make everything more exciting, more grandiose, and bigger than it really is—probably 'cause I can't be. Luckily, today was the last letter. So to tell the truth, I'm kind of glad it's over, for now.

But what's next, I wonder.

Leslie and I play a game called Major League. Kurt and I made it up years ago, for all the times when we got bored, usually when Mom went to the therapist and couldn't find a babysitter. The cheapest shrink in our old town was over at the community college, and Mom had to pick us up from school right before her appointments. So Kurt and I passed the time we waited by peering in dorm windows with binoculars, hoping to glimpse some skin.

"Ford Focus," I say, fixing the back windshield of one of the parked cars in my sights. "First base." A T-shirt flies up where we can see it between the front seat headrests.

Leslie and I make wagers on how far along each couple has gotten—if they're running the bases or slouching in the bull pen. We have Leslie's expensive flashlights, too, which are so powerful, they could help us pick out spots on the moon if we felt like it.

"You're joking," Leslie says, pushing me aside. "Look at him. He's got second base written all over him."

About twenty cars hide in the trees, half submerged so that their back ends stick out into the clearing, open targets. I sweep the windows, forcing head after head to dive for cover behind the seats.

"Check out the ugly Plymouth," Leslie says, wiggling her beam on a minivan.

Our glowing tunnels meet and join in midair, like they're in a mating dance courtesy of Energizer. Then we swoop down to illuminate the interiors of the ugly Plymouth with a sudden burst of light.

Inside the minivan a single shape splits into two separate bodies, and I catch a leg here, an arm there, wads of clothes cramped in the corner of the dashboard. The van doesn't rock yet, but it will.

"What do you think?" Leslie says.

"Third base," I say, drawing out a long breath of wonder. Third bases are tough to come across.

After a few more rounds, Leslie quits, and she leans back against the windshield with her arms behind her head, looking up at the stars. Every five minutes or so, the telescope dishes groan and turn clockwise on their pedestals. Somehow planet Earth seems a million miles away, as though we're marooned on an asteroid, all alone but together.

"Arty," she says, without even moving her eyes from the vast purple sky, "I've been wanting to ask you something for a couple days now."

"What?" I say.

"I want you to go to the dance with me this Thursday," she says. "Would you do that for me?"

"What dance?" No dances ring a bell.

"You know, the one they've been pushing all month," she says, folding her arms across her chest. "Haven't you seen the posters? I'm pretty sure it's a big deal."

I vaguely recall a flyer that featured a dancing gorilla wearing go-go boots. Then I remember who gave me that flyer one afternoon on a busy school sidewalk: Rose Purdy.

"That's a dance?" I say.

"Among other things," she says. "I really want to go, and I want you to go with me. I think we should. It will be a good opportunity to meet people, Arty. I'm still pretty new here, and I need to meet more people. That's why I want you to go with me."

I understand what she means. I've never been much good at meeting people, and I remember how shitty life was when I first started going to school here. The only people who ever even looked at me were those who wanted to know why I am the way I am. It's probably the same when you're so smart, or so hot, or so whatever. People treat you like that one sad puppy everyone visits in the pet store but no one wants to take home.

One of her thighs rests against mine, and the weight feels so good that I don't want to move. As much as it confuses me, I know I like this girl. There is no one reason why. But most of the time when I'm with her, I feel like I do when I'm in this field, with ice cream on my tongue and a lightness in my head. A fearless feeling.

"Yeah, I'll go," I say. Then I decide to give her something that I never thought I'd show anyone else in the world. "I made this for you." I take out my wallet and unfold the small sheet of paper tucked under my school ID.

"What is it?" she says.

"It's a list of the things I like about you."

She flattens the paper on the car hood and reads all nineteen things from top to bottom, taking her time:

THINGS I LIKE ABOUT LESLIE
(IN NO PARTICULAR ORDER)

- Looks great, even when she's sweaty and red after working out
- Wild eyes (in a good way)
- Sneaks an orange into the movie theater and then peels it in the dark
- Laughs with more energy than anyone else, like she's being electrocuted (in a good way)

- Mom might actually like her
- Sometimes she picks things up off a store shelf, and instead of paying at the register, she leaves cash on the empty spot on the shelf, then walks out the door
- Has a Viking Ice Cream takeout menu in her glove compartment
- Says she feels like eating something for dinner, then reads up on how to make it and makes it
- Speaks sexy German when she's on the phone with her dad
- Reads romance novels before bed, even though she calls them crap
- Has a personal website where she shows her home movies in streaming video
- Doesn't pay for everything, even though she has more money than me
- Likes gangsta rap
- Taught me how to downhill ski in the flat backyard on a hot Friday afternoon
- Actually listens when I talk
- Thinks my dad's a creep
- Goes to garage sales every weekend, and always buys something
- Knows everything
- Could hang out with anyone she wants but hangs out with me

A fluctuating smile-frown wobbles across her face. "That's so sweet," she says. It's enough. That list is the closest thing I'll have to writing her poetry. I'm glad she has it; otherwise it would wind up in the bottom of a drawer somewhere, and that's no place for your feelings.

"What's that?" Leslie says as she points into the tangled tree branches where the lights of Viking Ice Cream break through in scattered bits and pieces.

We shine our flashlights into the undergrowth and spot a figure running toward us—stumbling, actually. As the person closes the distance, I hear him calling out. I know who it is when the huge, wrinkly dinner plate ears come into view.

"Fight!" the kid I call Dumbo shouts for all to hear. He proceeds to trip over a couple making out in a rolled-up blanket on the ground. Surprised shouts rise up from the tall grass, mixed with a panicked, "Sorry, sorry."

Immediately upon hearing the word *"fight,"* some of the idling cars back out and crunch along the gravel toward the Viking parking lot. Not one to miss out on the action, Leslie jumps from the Jetta and starts picking her way through the trees. I have no choice but to follow. We emerge under the tilted lampposts by the Viking Dumpsters, where overturned barrels leak rainbows of spoiled ice cream into the gutter. A small huddle of kids stands there watching.

My breath catches in my throat when I see what's going on. I feel Leslie's slender arms wrap around my body from behind, encircling me like the harness on a roller coaster, squeezing.

Under the parking lot glow, a gigantic kid sits by the front doors of the ice-cream parlor, leaning against the outside wall like a dead curled-up bug. On either side of him are the frozen-cake display case and the rolling sundae-toppings cart that they bring out when the weather is nice. Both of them sit abandoned by customers too nervous to approach. In one meaty hand the kid holds a brown paper bag lamely concealing a bottle.

A skinny man in a dress shirt and clip-on tie, who I recognize as the manager of Viking Ice Cream, stands over the kid. He tries to keep his voice down, but the crowd is so quiet, we can hear every word. "I told you to leave," he says. "You've been drinking, and if you don't get lost, I'll have to call the police to come re-move you."

Parents and children stand far back to give the two of them plenty of room. They watch, as I do, as the manager tries to strut his stuff. He's not much older than the rest of us, probably some college dropout. It takes him a second to realize that he's still wearing his plastic Viking Ice Cream helmet, which he quickly snatches from the top of his head and drops to the concrete.

"I can do what I want!" the big kid yells back, and his voice cracks. "This is a public place."

"No, it's not," the manager says. "This is a private place of business, and you are disturbing the customers." He is trying to pretend that the gathering spectators are not really gathering.

"I just want to sit here," the big kid says, "around people."

"I'm sorry," the manager says, opening his hands. "Fridays are our busiest nights, and there is no loitering allowed. If you intend to buy ice cream, then do it and be on your way. If not, then go. You're making a scene."

"You want me to buy something?" the big kid says, and he leaps to his feet, only to wobble a few steps to one side and nudge the toppings cart off the sidewalk. The manager can't get away fast enough, and his escape bound looks like some elaborate jig, all knees and elbows. "Here," the big kid says as he rams his free hand into his pants pocket. He brings out a handful of loose change, which he then chucks in the manager's face.

A few girls in the crowd gasp, and I can see that events have taken a fateful turn. But this time I can't see what's coming next. It happens too fast.

Flinging the brown paper bag and its bottle to the ground, the big kid grabs the frozen-cake display case and shoves it into the toppings cart. The cart tips, crashing to one side and peppering nearby onlookers with chocolate sprinkles and nuts. Peeled bananas shoot by my feet like loosed torpedoes. The cake display cracks open, and two plastic scoops of fake white ice cream come loose from the top of a cake that says *Have a Grand-Slam Birthday!* in purple icing. Reaching down, the big guy snags one of the scoops before it rolls away. It's decorated to look just like a baseball, and it looks heavy. The big guy winds up. I think he has tears in his eyes as he pitches that single scoop of fake ice cream at Viking's big window, whipping it with so much force that it fractures the glass into a spiderweb of cracks. Then he takes off.

Dumbo, who has regained his composure, sprints up behind us and doubles over to wheeze.

"What happened?" Leslie says. Her face beams more excitement than concern as she picks a single candied cherry from her hair—a stray bullet from the toppings cart.

"That huge dude has been sitting there for an hour," Dumbo says. "He's been yelling at everybody that comes in the door. I think he's wasted."

"Unbelievable," Leslie says.

"The guy's crazy," Dumbo says.

"He's not crazy," I say, my heart sinking. "He's my brother."

"*That's* your brother?" Leslie says. "That's Kurt?"

People shout at Kurt as he runs across the parking lot, and a few angry men even seem ready to go after him. Yet, off he goes to wherever it is he goes, his secret lair where no one, not even I, can touch him. Together Leslie and I watch the hulking mass of my twin slip into the safety of the trees. He scrambles, hunched, like now he's the monster and I'm the bloodthirsty villager in the horror movie, holding my burning torch above my head and ready to lead the hunt.

After the crowd disperses and the mess gets mopped up, Leslie and I walk back to the field in the pitch black under the prickly pine trees. We climb into the Jetta without a word and head for home. I don't talk during the ride, but I can tell she's checking up on me from time to time, a flickering in the corners of her eyes. When we say good-bye, she gives me a hug instead of a kiss on the forehead. It's a weird feeling, like she's dropping me off at a friend's house or something—like I'm a kid going to a slumber party.

I watch the car speed off toward the middle of town, and when I look down, I see a few traces of ice cream sticking my fingers together. My fingertips smell like peanut butter, so I lick them clean.

As I jiggle the keys in the front door, a movement by the garage snags my attention. For a second I think it's Leslie coming back. Maybe she forgot to tell me something important; I don't know what, but something, like a list of things she likes about me. It could happen.

I almost feel sorry for Rose Purdy as the motion-detecting lamp above the porch switches on and blasts her with a white spotlight. Mom installed that sucker when we first moved in, just in case Dad tried to pull the old stalker trick and show up sporting his own bottle in a brown paper bag.

Rose blocks her face with an outstretched hand and waves me over into the darkness by the bushes. "Turn that damn thing off," she says. Instead, I shuffle a few steps to our crooked porch swing and sit down. My shoulders ache, and my eyes itch, and all of a sudden I feel so tired, like when you get up too fast and get the dizzies.

Rose scoots around Mom's car and then climbs over the railing, landing right next to me on the porch swing. She is not a small girl, and the chains groan as she wiggles her butt into a comfortable groove. Her jean jacket reeks of smoke.

"How you holding up, big guy?" she says. For once the sarcasm seems gone from her scratchy voice.

"Okay," I say. She carries a tote bag over one shoulder, her name embroidered in the mesh and circled by darting pink-and-purple butterflies. "What are you doing here?"

"Just making the rounds," she says. "Checking up on cases in the neighborhood. I heard you delivered that last letter and everything. Congratulations, I knew you had it in you."

She takes out a pack of girlie cigarettes, the thin, long kind with colorful stripes, and she lights one up. A puff of smoke bobbles into the air as she burps. "You've got your shit together, Moore, at least as far as I see it. I've got to go three blocks over here in a minute and put the smack down on Darryl Pinkus. I'm helping to keep his uncle from feeling him up, if you know what I mean. But the kid ain't easy to work with. Won't follow directions. It's like trying to push a parked car. But not you. You know what you want to get out of all this."

"You mean like what Kurt did over at Viking?" Only now does that scene of baseball ice cream and broken windows make some sort of sense. How I made Kurt freak out with my last letter, and all the others before it.

Rose tucks her chin into her neck and laughs quietly, the kind of laugh that mostly comes out your nose. "Yeah, I heard about that. Pretty easy, isn't it? Screwing with a dude's heart? I've done my share of that, all right."

"I got him pretty good, didn't I?" I say. The night air is cold even though it's almost summer, and bugs crowd the porch light. Neither one of us seems to want to look at the other.

"You're one of the best, Arty," she says. "A real storyteller. I've never met anyone who can make shit up like you can. Not even Jack." The corners of her mouth turn up into a smile, the kind I would never have imagined possible from a girl with slashes of dirt on her cheeks and a switchblade in her pocket.

"This is for you," she says. Thrusting an arm into the tote bag, she takes out a flat brown envelope the size of a place mat. "I just finished it a couple hours ago. A masterpiece, if you ask me."

"What is it? Section C?"

Rose stops cold. "What are you talking about?" she says.

"Section C of the red notebook," I say. "You know, there's a divider but no pages."

"It's a screwup," she says so fast I can hardly make it out. "Someone screwed up. There's no section C."

If she were anyone else, I wouldn't believe her for a second, but Rose is not just anyone else. "What is it, then?" I say.

"Phase two," she says. "Taking it to the next level." She stands up and stretches; I hear bones click and pop. "Make me proud, pip-squeak."

Then, just like that, she bolts, an angular shadow leaping from the porch and stretching down the long sidewalk.

I sit alone on the porch swing and rock back and forth as I think. I take Rose's letter out of the envelope and read it. Then I read it again. I sit there thinking until I fall asleep, and the sun comes up, and I find my keys still dangling in the doorknob.

AGAINST THE ROPES

 THE SCHOOL NEWSLETTER OF

THE FILLMORE HIGH SCHOOL BOXING TURTLES

"A turtle only makes progress when it sticks out its neck."
—Anonymous

WEEK OF MAY 30–JUNE 5

🐢 This week! June 3rd! Get blitzed on FUN! Come party with your friends at the school casino party with a "Circus Love" theme. Clown around! Walk the tightrope! Tickets: $24/each.

🐢 WOWEKAZAAM: For all your costume and party needs. Ever want to wear someone else's old clothes from the 1970s? Well, now you can. This and much, much more.

🐢 Stay alert! Have information about the horrific demise of our beloved Millie the Boxing Turtle? Remember, good colleges like honest students. Report all tips to a teacher or to Principal Malone.

Need a stepping stone to a career in reality television? Take part in channel twelve's honest and unstaged student panel discussion about the recent events surrounding our beloved Millie the Boxing Turtle. For scheduling and audition information e-mail Peggy: peggyz@channeltwelvesouthworth.net.

HALL PASSING

The next day I nod off in class and dream about Kurt pitching that fake scoop of baseball ice cream. As it smashes through my bedroom window and peppers the walls with glass, I jolt awake off my desk.

My biology teacher, Mr. Forke, stands over me, hovering a foot from my face.

Kurt's bellow pounds through my brain.

Mr. Forke stares at me for a long time, then strides back to his desk to continue the lecture from where he left off. The class laughs at me, another opportunity to disregard Mr. Forke and his riveting lesson on zygotes. Stick a Forke in me, I'm done.

I should have stayed home today. The other students, however, seem glad I came. It's weird, but it's like they can't get enough of me. And they all seem genuinely pleased that I've made friends with the new girl. They must think that because she can make friends with the mutant, then they probably have a shot at her, too. Like the pretty girls won't have to feel so unpretty, and the suave guys won't have to feel so uncomfortable, and the nerds won't have to feel too smart when she's around. I've broken new ground without even knowing it.

After a year of being nobody, I'm now in the public eye. Today high fives rain down on me as I walk the halls. Guys in letter jackets want to rub my head for luck at every turn. Girls wave and giggle and rattle their moneymakers. Is it a joke? I can't tell. Gus Van Mussberger traps me by the chem lab and plays a riff on the air guitar. He says it's from a song he wrote himself called "Arty Rocks My Rocks." In the old days hulks like him would flick boogers at me when I stood at my locker for too long.

I can't find a square foot of privacy. Not by the broken drinking fountain on the second floor, or even behind the retractable gym bleachers. Some knucklehead always waits with a "What's up?" or an excited "Party Arty, man," as soon as he spots me coming. It's funny because nobody ever wanted to know me before.

I walk in circles between classes, up stairs, down halls, down stairs, along the front trophy case, and inside the auditorium. Every time I close my eyes, I see Kurt breaking and bashing the ice-cream shop windows. His muscles, tendons, and veins pushing up against his pockmarked skin like some baby alien about to bust from his guts. I swear he had tears in his eyes.

Staring at the floor, I hardly notice the figure aiming at me from the elevator. Kid with No Legs speeds smoothly over the tile in his robotic chair like an Olympic figure skater, carving graceful arcs in the floor polish. Smiling is a chore for him, I can tell. His face twitches so violently that it hurts me to watch it. One of his hands convulses to mimic a pistol, and he pretends to shoot with one crooked finger, like, "Here's looking at you, kid!" Like we're a couple of guys out on the town, mixing it up, trying not to get in each other's way.

My brain seems to swell in my skull, and the cinching tightness makes me dizzy. For the only time all day, or maybe ever, I hurry off to my next class.

It's in my fifth-period government lecture that I really start tumbling downhill fast. Maybe it was how Kid with No Legs seemed to think we were buds, or the way some people glanced at me from under their eyelids as they passed on the way outside for lunch. There's something else buried in all the attention, and only now have I picked up on it. They're tracking me. Keeping tabs.

The pins glint like glossy red stars in the weak fluorescent lighting. The letter *A,* for Affront.

Two rows back Kraft Cheesy hunches over his notebook, doodling. The sun hits his pin and reflects upside-down *A*'s along the wall.

Soljah, one desk over, with her hair beaded in plastic jewels and a letter *A* pinned to her Cleveland Rockers scrunchie. She lip-synchs to the song in her earphones and checks me out over her sunglasses.

With his bony butt against the far back wall, Smithers uses a file to sharpen his fingernails into deadly weapons. A gold pendant rests on the notch at the base of his throat, a gleaming *A,* which fits perfectly over the groove like a plug.

They're everywhere.

I want the image out of my mind, that instant replay—Kurt throwing change in that guy's face; trails of white ice cream running alongside spinning nickels; mashed hot fudge and bananas on the oily concrete.

Beads of sweat trickle into my eyes and make them sting. My stomach shrivels and rolls over like it's playing dead.

I see Kurt hurl that baseball scoop at the ice-cream shop window.

I need the bathroom. My head hammers, joining forces with the acid burn in my stomach. Lips dry. Jets of spit fill the back of my mouth. I'm gonna barf.

I see Kurt stagger, a brown bag in his hand, gooey black fudge sticking to the soles of his shoes.

Suddenly I push away from my desk. Mr. Spur shoots me a curious look. But I leave him there and dash through the open door and then across the hall. As I hit the bathroom door, I taste the first burps of puke bubble up.

I stumble to the counter and turn on the middle faucet full blast, splashing water all over my face. A jammed urinal flushes endlessly in the corner of the room.

My stomach contracts violently, like a soda can crushed in some guy's fist. I make for the first stall, but it's a bad choice—someone left a surprise in that one. Stall number two has no door; so that leaves stall number three for me—third stall's the charm. I rush inside and fall to my knees.

Please, let this be over.

I vomit, and it feels like an elbow to the insides.

Then as quickly as it started, it's over. My stomach shivers, and I rest my head, feeling the chill of the porcelain against my face. A bitter chemical taste lingers in my spit.

As I slump there, an idea occurs to me. I take Rose's manila envelope out of my back pocket and hold it over the toilet. I've carried it with me all day. I had no choice. It hangs crumpled like an accordion over the settling Tidee Bowl surf. I reach to flush.

"You look tired," a voice says.

I turn my head to the side and see Kerouac standing in the stall doorway, smoking a cigarette. His torn white T-shirt says I LOVE MY PARENTS in blue iron-on. A friendly smile crosses his face, like he's going to validate my parking ticket for free or something.

"You could say that," I say. "Try sleeping on a porch swing."

He shakes his head. "I had you pegged, Arty-man," he says. "I figured you for a puker. But that ain't a bad thing." I don't have the strength to respond. The porcelain seems to pulsate, so cool against my cheek.

"All out?" he says. Leaning over he examines the toilet bowl. "I was a puker, too, you know."

"Congratulations," I say. I glance around in the splattered bowl half expecting to discover my internal organs caught up in some gruesome synchronized swim. But no, just ice-cream toppings and doughnuts. Lots and lots of doughnuts.

"Hey, man," Kerouac says. His soft voice sounds different, caring, not the same as the voice he uses with the others, with his brotherhood of factory freaks.

"What?" I say. "What's your big news?" I'm so sick of feeling bad about my life.

"Don't throw the letter away," he says in a droning voice, like a hypnotist's. My teeth throb from the roots out, seeming to rattle against the toilet bowl.

"Don't throw that letter away, man," he says again.

"What do you care?" I say.

"Trust me," he says. His cigarette filter smolders near its end. Oily black stains cover the web between his fingers. "I care."

I lean back against the stall wall and slide to the floor. My stubby legs stick out. They look so much like some little kid's, with the cute blue jeans, the red-and-white-striped sneakers. It occurs to me that I've worn this outfit since I was nine. *Nine years old.*

Not the exact clothes, really, but the outfit—the size medium shirt, jeans with the twenty-three-inch waist, the size three sneakers. This is my uniform, and it's not even mine. I'm almost positive this old green rugby shirt was once Kurt's, his hand-me-down from five years ago.

Sitting here, legs splayed, I think I can make out a rip from where the jeans got caught on a playground swing. And that burn hole on the cuff of the right shirtsleeve, it just might be from the candle that rolled off the cake at our tenth birthday party. Back when both of us were a medium, with a twenty-three-inch waist and size three sneakers.

This weird feeling buzzes over me, and at first I'm scared I'll heave again. But this pain is different, and it opens my guts, expanding into that empty space left behind by all those doughnuts. Tears fall from my chin to the front of my old green shirt.

My backbone shakes the wall, and I squash my hands over my eyes. Five years and everything is the same. I don't care that Kerouac waits beside me, because it's a good cry, clean and easy, not even worthy of a tissue.

Eventually he kneels down next to me on one knee and offers me a cigarette. I turn the pack away, and he smiles as though he knew I would but wanted to show how much he cares by offering. "I know just how you feel," he says. A chunk of ash plunks into the toilet, and he reaches over and flushes. He takes out a Handi Wipe and rips it open, then hands it over, practically wiping my burning forehead for me.

"I don't know if I can do it," I tell him. "This letter's too much, man."

"Yeah," he says. His face stays as solid and unrevealing as some big mountain carving. "I know you're scared. But I'll tell you what. Keep going this way, and you'll be scared until you're like sixty or something, and then one day you'll look at your watch and realize you've been living that way your whole life." He pulls the Handi Wipe out of my hand without asking and drops it into the gurgling bowl. "That's no way to live," he says. "You gotta get away from that thumb you've been wriggling under."

I know he's right. I need to hurt Kurt, if only to remind him that I'm not his human target, that I'm not nine anymore.

I struggle up off the floor with Kerouac's help, and he dusts off my pants, checking for vomit. He makes a swipe over my shoulders and then straightens my shirt, buttoning a button and turning the corners of the collar out. Somehow another cigarette made its way into his mouth along the way, and he swirls it around like a lollipop. He unrolls some toilet paper and hands it to me so I can blow my nose.

I hear crowds in the hallway now. My body steadies; no more vibrations and trippy shafts of light. Even the sourness in my stomach seems to have lifted.

Kerouac flips that copy of *On the Road* from his back pocket and thumbs through the worn, beaten corners of the pages. "You'll come out of this mess in one piece," Kerouac says. "I promise." The dirty pages make a buzzing sound against his thumbnail.

"Do you even keep promises?" I say.

"You'll have to wait and see," he says.

Focused, I look at the door. "You coming?"

"I'll go this way," Kerouac says. He unlocks the bathroom supply closet with a key on his ring of keys and walks inside. Boxes of industrial-strength disinfectant spray hog the floor, and up in a high cubbyhole, a selection of mops hang like they're on a gun rack.

"Do you pay rent around here or something?" I say.

He smiles and waves his cigarette like he's writing cursive with the lines of smoke. "I've got a little deal with Curly, the janitor," he says. His shape slowly melts into the lumpy shadows of trash cans and cleansers until nothing's left but an undistinguishable gloom.

I wait a few minutes after he's gone and then walk into the closet myself. I can't find him anywhere, and there's no door or passage or anything in the wall. Just a pile of snapped cigarette butts.

Then I hear a metallic bonging sound, and I glance up toward the ceiling. There, disturbed dust falls slowly through the slits of a ventilation duct, and I hear the sound again: the soft scrape of Kerouac's boots against the air shafts.

At the end of the day, I head home along the penny parade route. Few kids seem part of the caravan this afternoon, and the penny parade must be on tour, because no cars show up to pelt the sidewalks. Of the three cars that do pass, only one of them slows to fire a high-powered squirt gun at this skinny boy with sideburns. Other than that, it's a nice stroll in the piercing sunlight. It feels great to be out in the world again.

When I get home, I hop the steps and reach to swing the door open, but then freeze with a hand outstretched. Voices seep through the wood and screen. Then the last sound I expected to hear: Mom and Kurt sharing a chuckle in the kitchen. What's *she* doing home?

I take my usual position on the top stair and listen. A mosquito lands on my arm, but I don't smack it.

I concentrate hard on the sound from the kitchen, and I quickly realize that Mom's the only one chuckling. Kurt is with her, but silent. Besides, I don't think I even remember what his laugh sounds like.

Mom reads a movie review out loud, probably from behind an afternoon bowl of her favorite hippie grain cereal. The spoon tinkles against the edge of the garage-sale china.

"'Flaunton is so uncomfortable with his role that for the entire third act he appears to be walking around with the cardboard packaging still in his underwear,'" she reads. "'The best advice for him, after two such films to his credit, is to recommend tranquilizers, or to simply slap him upside the face between every take. One way or another, he needs to figure out what he's doing in front of the camera in the first place.'"

No response from Kurt.

"What do you think?" Mom says. "Should we see it?"

"No," Kurt says.

"It'll be fun," she says. "We'll get out of the house; we'll have dinner, make a night out of it."

I watch the mosquito on my arm as it finds a good spot to start sucking. I can't remember the last time Mom and I made "a night out of it."

"Can't you just give me money or something?" he says.

"What, and miss out on all the quality time?" she says. She's reaching; I can hear it in her voice. "Don't you want to go on a date with your mom?"

"Hell no," he says. I can't help but wonder when Boy from the Planet of the Apes got so polite.

"Maybe we'll go play minigolf or something," Mom says. "You still like minigolf, right?"

"Not since I was, like, seven," Kurt says. He's boiling mad, the anger backing up behind his words like water against a crumbling dam.

"Well, I'll come up with something," she says. "I want you to know how proud I am."

"Whatever," he says.

I don't have a clue what they're talking about. Are they going steady now? Has Kurt wowed Mom with a newfound ability to write his own name? It's not fair. All I want right now is to make fun of some stupid movie with my mom over a bowl of muesli. More than anything in this whole crappy world.

"Honey, talk to me," Mom says. The good humor is gone from her voice, replaced with worry.

"Damn it," Kurt says quietly, wrestling the words out of his mouth. I can almost see him. This is what always happens; his anger makes it so he can hardly even talk.

"Kurtis?"

There's a growl from Kurt and a squeal as a chair gets thrown back away from the table. Two fists land on the kitchen counter with a bang, sending a tremor up through the walls of the house. Silverware jumps, and something, maybe a broom or a mop, falls cracking to the linoleum.

Then he shouts things that aren't words, just noises.

"Oh, honey, don't," Mom says, almost in a whisper. A chair squawks as she stands up.

"What'd I do?" Kurt says. "I don't get it."

"Sometimes people just kick other folks out on their asses," Mom says. "No one knows why. Remember—if some girl could do that to you so easily, then you probably don't want to know her in the first place. Come on; don't make that face."

There's a sound, like a hiccup, coughed tears, and I hear Kurt's voice crawl out. I can't understand what he says, but he strangles some sobs with Mom's shirt. I'm pretty sure he's crying. Good.

I check back with the mosquito on my arm, and he's got a huge bellyful of blood as he stands there sucking. So I mash the little bastard into jelly.

I pull the mangled manila envelope from my back pocket. TO PRINCIPAL MALONE shines on the front in black ink. That Rose Purdy, at it again. After last night I probably know every word of this by heart. Let's see.

I tune the voices to background static and then open the envelope, removing the single sheet of stationery that's tucked inside. And even though I've read it a million times, I read it again:

To Principal Malone,
If I was interested in Millie the Turtle,
I'd be interested in Kurt Moore. I hear
his locker holds the truth. Proof.
A concerned party

The Mary Fielder letters were just a taste test compared to this. He won't know what hit him.

That's *my* mom in there.

Big Feeling

Four feet two inches tall.

I sit in my bedroom closet, straddling my desk chair underneath the bent and rusty nails meant to be coat hooks. I stare at the tape measure on the wall. My feet don't touch the ground. A layer of dust coats the cardboard boxes from our move like drifts of dandelion fuzz.

I look down at the two hormone cartridges in my palm. They weigh as much as a couple of quarters, maybe. That's all. It's pretty stupid to think that something this small can really help you, can change your body and change your life. The needle points at the ceiling. I flick the end and make it quiver, mostly because cool people always do that in the movies. It doesn't look so cool, anymore. Kind of sad, really. It looks pathetic.

"You know the drill," I say. Then I wait, alone in the dark and the dust. The half-open door slices a rectangle of light across the floorboards.

"Think of something."

I try.

I think about Dad, and when he left. How we found the back door of the apartment open, the appliances stacked on top of one another with the cords wound into knots for easy handling. That, and the note on the counter. Not even a genuine letter but a page ripped from one of those desktop day calendars, messy with scribble. The police were sure he and some buddies had planned to come back and take everything.

Good thing Kurt and I got home early from hockey practice.

Mom sat me down that very night and told me we'd get to the bottom of this whole not-growing thing. A year and a half later I was diagnosed, and for six months I've been sticking myself with needles.

"Think of something good," I say.

I sit in the musty closet and take deep breaths of dust. I push the plunger hard. It hurts a little. I push harder.

MONKEY SEE, MONKEY DON'T

W"hat school has dances on a Thursday night, anyway?"

It's seven o'clock, and we clomp around in my third-floor bedroom, with Mom in her cross trainers and me in my rubber ape feet. The costume shop's bright blue garment bag sits in a crumpled pile on my desk, uncomfortably close to the secret red binder. The binder looks harmless enough, sandwiched between two books called *Stranger in a Strange Land* and *Journey to the Center of the Earth,* books that I got for free from a box on the curb, and that look really damn boring.

Mom zips up my rubber pecs, scowling, ditching her cigarette in the art-class-sculpture-gone-bad that sits on the dresser. "And look at the ass on you, kid. Are you a baboon, a gorilla, what? I've seen both, and you're neither."

I love my mother. She shakes her head in bewilderment, exhaling a tornado of smoke that rides the wind from the open window.

I'd be lying if I said life was perfect. Perfection, I'm afraid, is Hollywood fantasy. I'm going to a school dance with the girl of my dreams, exactly what I've always fantasized about—plunging necklines and slow dances, a girl with a body like a centerfold and a brain like a search engine. But lurking around at the back door of my mind is this growing unease, like I know all that razzle-dazzle's only for show. That I'm still fantasizing, and I just haven't woken up yet.

I can't stop thinking about phase two of The Plan, as I've come to call it.

Mom and I haven't seen Kurt all afternoon. He comes and goes randomly now. I figure he must be off in that secret place he always rushes to at the first hint of trouble. Whatever he's doing, it's driving Mom to the edge with worry. The last couple of nights, she's stayed up to wait for him in little stakeouts that didn't pay off. Her tired face looks a bit like bad milk, yellowing, wrinkling, lumpy in places it wasn't lumpy before.

She's right about my butt, though. The prosthetic monkey ass sticks out about a foot more than it needs to, throwing the outfit's already shaky authenticity into a shambles. Leslie went to this costume store and picked out a pair of costumes without even asking my opinion. It seems that this high school dance is not only a dance but also a costume party and a casino night.

"I don't know why that girl picked this costume," Mom says. Her hands pinch my monkey lips as she screws the head onto my shoulders. My line of sight matches up with the eyeholes, and I catch my reflection in the bedroom mirror. I look like a leprechaun with a life-threatening skin condition.

"Sick," Mom says, more to herself than to me. "Truly hideous."

"It's my Kurt suit," I say, and I do a little jig right there on the floorboards.

Mom's face scrunches up like she's about to get pissed, but then it softens. "That's my Arty," she says. "The funny little monkey."

My crazy simian grin smiles back from the mirror, and I forget for a second that it's me under all that hair and rubber.

"You really want me to take a picture of this?" she says. The Nikon whirls from its strap on her wrist. I think it still has film in it from our trip to Florida a couple years ago. The summer Kurt's chin broke out, our last family vacation ever—the "we're still a family" raise-our-spirits vacation we took after Dad beat it.

Mom had stayed close to the hotel bar. Kurt and I had already begun jockeying for her affection.

"This might be the second most humiliating thing a Moore has ever done," Mom says. She plays with the camera, peeping backward through the lens and shaking it like a tribal charm. "Is this sucker even on?"

"The *second* most humiliating thing?" I say.

She smiles and snaps a candid shot of me scratching my monkey butt. "Well, the first most humiliating thing is more like a big collage of every idiotic thing your dad ever did. If we wanted to count those separately, he'd easily hog the top fifty humiliations all to himself.

"Now scare me, monkey," she says. "Go wild. Go apeshit. Make me cringe." The shutter clicks as she dances around mimicking a fashion photographer, directing me, squinting through her gray-rooted bangs.

I almost wish I could take my mom to this dance. What would I do without her?

Soon she drops the camera and plops onto my unmade bed. Her cigarette licks at its filter, so she lights another one and stares outside through the window, between the stirring curtains. The line of her mouth jumps around, unable to settle on one expression. I bet she's remembering things that hurt her, things that make her laugh sometimes, things that other times make her cry like she's about to die.

Probably the best perk of being so tiny is that I can curl up next to my mom just like I did when I was a little kid. So I sit down next to her and rest my head on her forearm. Her thick white legs look like marble, a hint of blue veins under the surface. The pendant I made spins around her neck, winding its silver cord.

"I know things have been hard, Arty," she says. "You've gotten knocked around a bit in life; that's for sure. I've always tried to be there for you the best I can, and I'm trying to be there more for your brother now, too. Honest. My hope is that when you guys look back on these years, you won't totally hate my ass."

I don't say anything, just soak up the warmth of her skin through the rubber and hair of my costume.

"You're a good kid, Arty," she says.

Good is not the word for me.

Through those ape eyeholes I see her face, lightly powdered, heavily glossed in eye shadow, rouge, and lip liner, and I miss her even though I see her all the time.

Unprepared, she looks down and finds my eerie monkey lips grinning up at her. She scoots a couple of butt-lengths away from me. "No kidding, kid; that is one serious car crash of a face you got there."

I check out the alarm clock and see that it's almost eight. "So I look okay, right?" I say. "She'll be here, like, any second."

"If you're going for hairy and terrifying, then you look fabulous," she says, and drops her shoulders. "I wish I knew more about this girl you're going with. I know you've been spending a lot of time with her, but, well, I still feel weird about it. I know I'm not always around, and if there were another way, I'd go for it without a thought. I might even get promoted soon. Better hours, better pay, more time with my guys." The air-conditioning clicks on with a stutter as Mom stands up and walks over to her purse on my miniature desk.

"This is a big night for you," she says. "I want to give you a couple things." I have trouble tracking her because my mask has the worst peripheral vision ever. She approaches, enlarging in the eyeholes, and I feel her press a square object into my palm. Whatever it is squishes in my fingers and makes a crinkling noise. I rub it for a second and then lift my hand to my face, before I understand.

My mom has just slipped me a condom.

In a reflex I whip that puppy across the room and into the wall, where it bounces off the laundry hamper and lands spinning on the floor. There it sits, ready to prevent pregnancy and the transmission of STDs.

My hand tingles, and I search to see if the condom left a mark. It was purple. *Purple.*

"What was that for?" Mom says.

"What was *that* for?" I say, confused. "Where did you get that?"

Mom drags on the cigarette and rolls her eyes. "I have a few, okay? Am I not allowed to have some sitting around just in case the world ends and a man comes knocking down my door?"

"Yes," I say. "Of course, you are." Then I start feeling sort of bad for acting like such a baby when I'm supposed to be showing how much of an adult I am, having a date with a girl and all.

Uncomfortable, she steps to my small chest of drawers and casually moves my stuff around: the square brown bottle of cologne, the tube of zit cream, the can of hair mousse with the grime around the nozzle.

"I know, I know," she blurts, sticking out her tongue. "Pretty stupid, huh? Blah. Stupid, lame Mom. What a joke. I guess I thought that's what moms do now, okay? When I went through puberty, your grandma got me a sex book from the church library. That's the best she could do. Shows how much I've learned."

Then she turns to me, pools in her eyes, teeth chomping her top lip uncontrollably. "You'd tell me if you'd seen your brother, right?" she says. Her voice slides into a weak scrape. "You wouldn't keep it a secret, would you? Because I know you have secrets, Arty. I know it."

"No," I say. I get up off the bed and take her hand. "I'd tell you, Mom." Though I know she and Kurt have secrets of their own.

"Good," she says. "I hoped so."

Suddenly her eyebrows jump up as though she just remembered something, and she fumbles in her jeans pocket for a small white box, which she brings out and shakes between her fingers.

"Is it something nasty?" I say, backing up.

She can't help but grunt with laughter before tossing the box in my direction. "It's something I found in your granddad's stuff last year. I think he'd want you to have it on your first big date, lover boy."

With trembling hands, I take the lid off the gift box and strip back the first layer of cotton. There, staring up like a magical eye, sits a polished silver drawer knob. A fake red jewel glitters in the center, and swirled around in the threads of cotton winds a metal cord, a lot like the one on Mom's necklace. I remember this. I had forgotten, but it comes back to me.

I must have made this for Grampa when I was young, and he never got around to opening it. Even the classy box and the squares of striated cotton look familiar. I'm glad I'm sitting, because my legs have gone numb. I take the amulet out of its nest and hang it around my neck. The knob weighs heavy and cold on my collarbone. This has to be the best gift I've ever given and gotten back again.

Mom watches with a giant exhausted smile, and I know that even though I'm a shrimp with a joke of a body, I must have inherited that great big grin, because I feel it break across my face. "Thanks, Mom," I say. She comes to me, and I hug her long lady legs.

Again I think about what I've done and what I plan to do. I think about the letter tucked under my belt. How its corners poke into my stomach. How it might change things more, probably for the worst. I think about what I'm going to do when I get to school. It makes me wonder who I'm trying to hurt, anyway.

A car pulls into the driveway. Mom glances up, listening with a face drained of blood and filled with hope. But when Leslie rings the doorbell, all hope of Kurt's return seeps from Mom's eyes, and she shouts, "Come in!" in a hoarse voice out the window. "Up in the attic!" We wait as the footsteps cross the hall, jump the first-floor steps, turn the corner, and climb the tower stairs.

The door flies open and Leslie appears, feathers clinging to her arms and legs, and a tail pointing out into the stairwell. She stands adorned in a six-foot-tall chicken suit, complete with rubber beak and googly black eyes. Under the enormous beak, her pretty face drips with sweat and her lipstick trails off from her lips and zigzags halfway across one cheek. Her cell phone earpiece dangles, the cord swinging in knots down her chicken breast.

"I'm here," Leslie says, gasping between words. "I didn't think I'd make it. Practice went long and Fred Eastman fell down a flight of steps."

"You're a chicken," Mom says. That's my mom, master of the glaringly obvious. She concentrates hard on Leslie, plucking her apart, not noticing the long ash about to fall from her cigarette.

"We've switched themes," Leslie says. Under her left wing she carries a shiny rectangular box with a logo embossed in silver.

"I don't see how this is going to work," Mom says, eyeing Leslie's plumage. "Aren't you supposed to be Tarzan or Jane or something?"

"I was inspired at the last second," Leslie says, and she moves to open the box with the shiny label. But her chicken wings prove unwieldy, and the contents cartwheel to the floor in a wave of tissue paper.

When she crouches down in hot pursuit, her mouth opens—to speak, or chirp, or whatever—and she finds the foil wrapper, the purple condom eye staring up at her. She creaks to a stop. So does my heart.

Like people do in every tense situation, we all freeze, a bunch of cowboys in the sand waiting for one person to yell, "Draw!" so the rest of us can come out with guns blazing.

And it's Mom who saves the day.

"Sorry, that's mine," she says, and bends over to pick up the condom. Shrugging, she throws Leslie a shy smile and shoves the purple thing back into her purse, where I will never have to see it again.

I've got to hand it to my mother. She sure knows how to save a hairy leprechaun from getting dumped by a giant chicken. Her eyes sparkle like trashy blue nail polish, and she ruffles my ape hair. Only a real friend would take a bullet like that.

CIRCUS LOVE

Mom stays in the doorway awhile with my monkey suit flung over one shoulder, and she waves until she darkens into nothing but a shape against the screen.

"Bianca did a great job on this chicken suit," Leslie says. "We'll have the best outfits there." She walks with the keys fanned out in her hand like a deadly throwing star. I look for her face inside that black hole of the chicken's mouth, but all I see are the whites of her green eyes.

"Who's Bianca?" I say.

"My designer," Leslie says, unlocking the Jetta with a beep of her key chain. "She overnighted the costumes from New York. I was afraid they wouldn't get here in time."

My new costume pinches around the armpits, and the white plastic fogs up faster than a bathroom mirror.

On the horizon a big top peeks high over the trees, a canary yellow tower skewering the moon. Never has our town seemed smaller, barely bigger than a rented circus tent. A flag unfurls from the topmost spire as a searchlight appears over the tree line and sweeps the low clouds. Leslie backs the Jetta out of the driveway and then hits the gas, and we tear up Pasture Road, north toward our date with demented destiny.

We soon come upon others who are speeding up the long, curving backwoods road. The trucks in front of us all find the same radio station and blast their stereos into one blended burp. Kids stick out from the sunroofs and lob empty beer cans at oncoming traffic. One sails at our windshield and Leslie swerves, her eyes focused on the tip of the circus tent, on the flags and banners. As we close in, the tent expands and quickly fills the entire windshield with bright yellow.

I really can't see much from my costume's single slanted eyehole. All I'm able to make out is Leslie at the wheel—her slender feathers, her feet tied into orange knee-high boots that were painted to look like claws. She cusses as she works the pedals, weaving to avoid the barrage of cans from the truck ahead of us. A kid dressed as the Green Lantern moons us from the back of a flatbed pickup.

I start thinking about Rose's instructions. *I can do this,* I tell myself. *I have to. Don't I?*

The sides of my costume seem to close in, and I am steamy, crazy hot. There's no air. I jab at the door locks and window controls, gasping for air, fumbling in my partial blindness.

Startled, Leslie turns to me and taps the brake pedal, sucking us against the seats and rebounding us back toward the dashboard. "What's wrong?"

"Do we have to go?" I say. "Do we have to go to this dance?"

"Yes, we have to go," Leslie says. "I've been planning this for weeks."

"You just came up with these costumes, like, yesterday." I say. I hate how her plans go one way, unalterable, divine law.

"Listen, I forked over a ton of money for this," she says. "I want it to go well. This is my real debut, Arty, and I need to make a good impression."

"You already have," I say. "People love you."

"I'm not talking about making friends, Arty," she says, adjusting her chicken head in the mirror and rubbing lipstick off her cheek. "Never mind. You wouldn't understand. Just try to have some fun, okay?"

But I'm in flames now, locked in this shell where I can't take a lungful of air to save my life. "What do you mean you 'forked over a ton of money'?"

She presses a tissue against her lips, blotting the brown color and at the same time rearranging the junk in her purse, all as she pilots the car into a parking spot with her knees. "This," she says, and her finger jabs at the yellow tent blocking the windshield. "I paid for all of it. You should have seen what they had planned before I came along. 'Night on the Mississippi.' Steamship gambling, Arty! Crepe paper and balloons. Guys in white-and-red-striped vests. The principal all done up like Mark Twain. No. Not at my school, Arty. Not if I can help it."

"Who cares?" I say. "Why do you even care? About everything? What's the big deal?" As my voice rises, an elephant emerges from a flap in the tent and lumbers through the mud. A man follows behind, shouldering a tranquilizer gun.

"Because," Leslie says, watching the elephant, "because of the secret."

"What secret?" I say.

"The secret of success," she says. "It's the family philosophy."

"And what's that?" I say.

Leslie cracks the door, and the interior light comes on, and before stepping out, she touches my hand, just like she did in the movie theater, and I remember liking the darkness for once then, as the smell of butter from Camilla's jumbo tub of popcorn dried on my fingertips.

"Always get noticed," Leslie says, keeping a straight face. "It's all that matters when you get down to it. Making an entrance." She takes my hand and looks down at me. "People notice you, Arty. And I like that."

Tugging me along, she steps into the grass of the football field. It feels like walking in a recurring dream, when you know bad things are just around the corner but you just can't stop yourself—and in you go.

Cars and trucks disgorge teams of kids and park haphazardly on the private lawns nearby. Tiki torches sprout curls of dark smoke in the entryway, where cops mutter into their headsets and balance atop their mountain bikes. We walk through all of it.

Cool air leaks through the cracks in my costume. I take big gulps of it. Moisture beads on the pearly plastic, and I smell myself slow roasting, shirt stuck to skin. Above our heads, giant searchlights cut across the sky and meet for a second in the clouds, dogfighting along the tree line.

Leslie pulls me along. "Come on, Arty," she says. "Pick up your feet."

The tent looms and its walls rustle, ropes wobbling in the breeze and stakes holding steady. Streamers in our green-and-white school colors line the cords. A red velvet carpet leads from the fifty-yard line to the front of the tent. Students cluster under the canopy and hand over tickets. Ms. Wessin operates the ticket booth, all dolled up in a daring miniskirt that shows off her dimpled legs. She tugs down on the hem every few seconds and glances around to see if anyone notices.

But no one cares about Ms. Wessin because all eyes are on *us,* and everyone hoots and squeals and barks like a dog. I close my eyes and let Leslie guide me one last time.

When we reach the ticket booth at the end of the red carpet, I open my eyes to a yearbook page of familiar and not-so-familiar faces.

"Get it—he's the egg and she's the chicken," a bystander explains. Actually, a boy dressed as Superman says it, shouting it to the bearded wizard on his right.

That's right: I'm wearing an egg costume built by a New York nutcase named Bianca.

The crowd ignites with laughter, spreading giggles across both sides of the red carpet. One boy decked out as an entire barbershop quartet, complete with dummies strapped to either side of him, starts clapping with his eight plastic hands. The whole mess of onlookers joins in until the applause grows positively thunderous.

Then I get the joke.

Which one of us came first, the chicken or the egg? Get it? It's so brilliant that I want to tear Leslie's chicken plumage off her back and shred it in my fists. You see, only I could be the egg: Boy with the Booster Seat, Baby Hands, Shot Glass, Footstool, Midget.

Arty. The only one small enough.

I hide inside my eggshell. The cool surface reminds me of the toilet bowl of that school bathroom, and I press my cheek against it.

Now I understand why Leslie and I are friends in the first place. Why this perfectly sized egg costume was probably just sitting around in her mansion waiting for its rightful owner. She always planned it to happen this way. In answer to that old question, the egg most definitely came first.

So we make our entrance. Leslie pulls me along through the gigglers. I squeeze her feathered hand so tightly, my muscles ache. I'm afraid to let go. Hers is the only girl's hand I've ever held.

UNDERCOVER EGG

Sometimes there are things a person needs to do. And most of the time, people forget the reason why they need to do them, only that they have to.

Take my dad, for example. I don't think he knew exactly why he had to steal the car and go, but he knew things would only get worse for everyone if he stayed. I think even Mom would agree with that one. And Grampa, why did he take me grocery shopping that day, even after doctors told him not to leave the house? There must have been something eating away at him, a fear of losing control that he tried to beat, but that put him on his back and crying in aisle seven.

I have no control. My body fights against me every hour of my life. It fights to stay small, and I make lists and come up with stories of what could be but won't ever happen. There is nothing good about being this way.

I hide in the fortune-teller's booth, and the rest of life flows around me. People in control in a world out of sorts. A pair of acrobats jitterbugs across the big top. The wind outside butts the walls of the tent, shaking the canvas, fighting to get in through the flaps. Standing on its hind legs, the elephant claps its front feet as the trainer bows with a flourish, sweeping his top hat low across the floor, not noticing that the men holding the restraints are being pulled off their feet.

I take off the top of my costume so my head sticks out again. In the dark no one can see my face, anyway.

In my spot by the fortune-teller's table, I can smell corn popping. The crystal ball sparks on the small round tabletop draped in silk. It bathes my white egg blue and makes my tears sparkle as they roll.

Looking through the crowd, I search for Leslie and catch her camped out beside the blackjack tables and the roulette wheel. Her feathers lie on the coat table by the shooting gallery. Now she wears a red satiny dress that's practically painted on. Vincent Nguyen stands next to her looking bored, not laughing at a single joke. Her fingernails dig into the elbow of his suit.

The acrobats spin over my head and gently brush hands, missing, then tumble down into the safety nets.

I slip outside before I start to cry even more.

I try not to think about anything except finishing my mission, following Rose's simple instructions to the letter. It keeps the sadness back, pushes me forward across the muddy field, which slurps hungrily at my shoes. The wind, picking up as I hit the sidewalk, tries to blow me away. Clouds darken and thicken over the tent spire. I keep moving.

When I reach the back doors of the school building, I find the handles latched with a chain. The shattered bulb of the outside light sparkles on the doormat, and in between the bits of frosted glass lies a red pin— the letter *A*. All according to phase two.

I take out the key Rose gave me and fit it into the padlock that holds the chain. It takes some twisting, but soon the bolt snaps, and the chain unrolls down the steps before I can rush to grab it. It rings like a bell choir in a bar brawl. I wait, silent. But there's nothing, not a rustle of bushes or a flash of searchlights.

Next thing I know, I'm inside the school, past the wide gray doors of the gym, then scaling the stairs to the skinny library corridor. My muddy shoes make sharp shrieks on the polished tile, kind of like the *wheh-wheh* string music in that movie *Psycho*.

I wish I could take the damn egg suit off, but removing it requires two people, and I'm only about half a person to begin with.

I know that the building is empty and that I'm alone. Rose promised me it would be. But I half expect someone to leap from an open doorway or dart from behind a drinking fountain as I round the corner.

I'm so hyped up that I almost don't hear the footsteps when they start.

They follow, rubber soles squeaking and echoing down the hallways same as mine.

A flashlight beam dots the pay phone across from the school store, flickering orange like the glow of a dying campfire.

It's too late to run, to hide. The steps sound heavy and huge, not just from some kid but from wide, thudding grown-up feet.

Then they're here. My stalker rounds the corner and his flashlight sweeps across my frightened face, turning the world into a dazzle.

The mystery man leaps back and shrieks, girlie style. I turn to run but lose control of my egg, awkwardly wobbling against a row of lockers and spiraling to the floor. My egg very slowly rocks to a standstill.

"Hey, you okay?" the guy says. The voice has a familiar high-as-a-kite ring to it.

"What are you supposed to be, a Ping-Pong ball or something?" he says.

"No, I'm not a Ping-Pong ball."

"Too bad; that would have been cool," he says. I only know two people who might say something like that, and one of them is back at the party dressed in satin and swapping spinach dip with Vincent the Tibetan Wonder Nut.

"Gus?" I say.

"What?" he says. The flashlight swivels up toward his face, and I'm hardly shocked to see Gus Van Mussberger dressed in an Iron Maiden T-shirt and eating a PayDay.

"What are you doing here?" I say.

With a showy move he probably rehearsed in front of a mirror, Gus stretches the neck of his shirt and flips the fabric inside out, showing me his red pin.

Another bloody *A*.

"You're with Rose and them?" I say.

"Sure," Gus says. "They helped me pass freshman year."

"What are you doing here?"

He looks at me like I've got my head screwed on backward. "How else did you expect to get this?" Then, from behind his back, he swings out an oversize wheeled trash can and scoots it between us. "I don't do any of the brainy stuff," Gus says. "Mostly the heavy work. You know—moving stuff, stealing stuff, breaking stuff."

He points to the tool belt hanging around his blubbery waist, and then swings his hips to make all the assorted screwdrivers and wrenches knock together like they're parts of a handyman wind chime.

"You do 'stuff'?" I say.

"Yeah, stuff," he says, nodding. Then he points down into the garbage bin. "You need a little help with this stuff, dude? It's heavy as hell."

I roll the trash can around toward the hallway light so I can see it better. What's inside takes my breath away.

"Framing someone's no good without the proof, eh?" Gus says. He seems very proud to be a part of all of this.

Millie the Boxing Turtle stares up at me from inside the depths of the black plastic trash bag. Or at least what remains of her: the decapitated head. Her stone eyes hold no expression, but the smile on her face remains the same as I remember. Still hard-ass and ready for anything. Poor Millie; she used to hide me on those hot days after school. She was cool.

I puff out the edges of the bag so I can't see her face anymore, and then Gus and I wheel her down the hallway and lift her carefully up the third-floor stairs, one step at a time. Whenever we hear a noise, we glance at each other, pause, then start moving again. Finally we touch her down at a row of freshman lockers and push her down the long, gray corridor to number 499.

I know for sure it's Kurt's because of the dents at the bottom, no doubt from angry kicks, and the faded Magic Johnson sticker slapped on crookedly near the number plate at the top.

I pull out Rose's crib sheet and find the locker combination. This single piece of paper holds every bit of critical Kurt information a person might need, from his social security number to his grade point average. I can't take my eyes off his height, which is listed at the bottom of the sheet as six feet three inches. That's even bigger than I had guessed.

Much to my surprise, Gus seems to be on top of things. I'm totally not. I can hardly concentrate on the combination. The digits keep blurring, and my whole body feels drowsy and slow. "Come on," Gus says. He crouches at the foot of the lockers, unwinding an extension cord that he plugs into an outlet by the water fountain. From his tool belt, he takes a handheld work lamp, and lighting it, slides it next to my shoes, so the snakelike neck gives me the best light. Looking down is like taking a peek at one of those eclipses you're not supposed to stare at.

"All we need to do is put Millie in there and you're done, dude. I'll get the head into the locker and you get that letter ready. We'll slip it under the principal's door on the way out. Then it's off to Bob Evans, baby."

Without my help Gus tips the trash can over on one side and crawls inside it. The legs of his dirty jeans wiggle around in a circle as he rolls over, corkscrewing his way into the tube with a bunch of loud gorilla grunts. I slide on the black gloves Rose gave me.

They're kiddie-sized, of course. I check on Gus, who's still rustling around inside the bag. I guess I just can't stand around and watch anymore.

As Gus works with the head, I pull the tip-off letter out from where it's folded under the back of my belt. The crinkled paper stinks from being strapped to my sticky skin. It smells like me, like my dirty laundry hamper or my gym bag. Will it give me away? Don't the police use special dogs to track these kinds of things?

At last I get the combination right and pop Kurt's locker door. A deflated basketball that's been propped against the door falls to the hallway floor. On the bottom of Kurt's locker lies a collection of buried schoolwork, forgotten food, cigarette butts, and squashed soda cans. A couple of recent issues of *Playboy* top the pile. I can't believe how gross his locker is, like the back room of an auto shop or something.

"The principal's gonna freak when he finds this puppy," Gus says. He works to roll Millie's head up into the locker. Like a robot I snap to life and grab hold of a jawbone, putting my back into it, lifting with every tiny muscle. Just as the head is about to drop inside, Millie's big goofy grin gets caught on either side of the locker door. It almost looks like she's smiling wider than before.

"This is supposed to fit, right?" Gus says.

"Don't ask me," I say. I would expect that some advanced geometry nerd working for Affront would have worked out these scenarios ahead of time. What kind of school resistance group is this, anyway?

"We sure this is the right head?" Gus says, bending over to take a look inside the empty trash can.

"Yeah," I say, "pretty sure."

After many attempts to jam the head into the locker, we finally give up and let it clunk loudly back to the hallway floor. Millie grins up at me, laughing at my stupidity.

But at least I still have *my* head. "Give me your hammer," I say to Gus.

"What for?" Gus says.

"Just give it to me."

"Whatever, man." He hands over the hammer.

Crouching down on the floor, I find a good grip on the hammer's cool wooden handle and then whack Millie a good one on the top of her head. A single chip flies off and bounces around the walls of the locker with a ricochet clang. I raise the hammer again and strike, and another chip zips by my cheek and slides along the ground. I stop for a second to survey my work, inspecting the turtle's caved-in skull—Millie has shrunk.

I can make the head fit. All she needs is a few more good sharp raps on the noggin, and I'm home free. I look up at the locker to size it up, and then cock back the hammer.

That's when I catch sight of Kurt's locker-door art. It steals my next breath and makes my chest tighten.

Up next to a two-page spread of some lingerie model hangs a folded photograph. It's of Mom and him and me, and from the looks of it, it was shot on that trip to Florida a few years back. I can tell by the co-conuts and our puffy sunburns.

I hold the hammer high, and it weighs, like, a million pounds in my hands. It almost hurts, it's so heavy.

I can't stop staring at that picture. It's like looking into some window. I can practically see the palm trees fanning us in the sway of tropical breezes. Oh yeah. We stand there like we do in every photograph, but different: Mom much thinner in her workout pants, a Popsicle in her fingers instead of a cigarette; Kurt is holding a boogie board that's as big as he is, smiling, white teeth and cinnamon-tan skin; and me, same as now but making some funny face with a streak of sand above one eye.

Seeing us taped to this locker door above a heap of rotting apple cores and girlie mags makes me feel funny, not so tired maybe. Strong. In control.

I bring the hammer down hard on Millie's left eye and it explodes. The shock wave dances up my arm and feels amazing. I raise the hammer and bring it down on the other eye, blinding her and almost blinding myself as tiny slivers fly everywhere.

This is what I think of Kurt and his family photo and his tropical breezes and his coconuts.

I smash Millie's big goofy grin, knocking out every turtle tooth.

This is what I think of his six feet three inches. This is what I think.

I crack her beak off with one swift blow that makes my wrist flash with pain.

When I'm done I crumple down in the ring of gray stone powder. Cuts on my face burn from where the bits and pieces backfired. But that's about all.

Gus stands back and surveys the final result. "Off with her head, man," he says. "That'll get his attention." He presses something against my chest—Millie's cracked right eye. "Every killer's got to take a trophy."

Then we hear clicks of shoes in the hallway.

I cradle the hammer in my hands.

"Arty, is that you?" a sweet voice says.

Leslie?

I think I might eggsplode.

TRIPPED

It always comes back to class. There's no escaping it, like Mom spinning those Exercycle pedals like a gerbil on one of those round plastic wheels going nowhere.

No matter what happens, I sit at a desk the next morning, again. Just another version of yesterday, or tomorrow, as though nothing ever happens, or changes, ever. Fridays come and Fridays go, but Ms. Wessin and her bleached mustache will always remain to make sure I never forget that life is one long and depressing haul.

My last-period American studies class fills the computer lab, and there aren't enough computers, so in the nearby corner some of us wait our turns, seated at a mob of desks that are turned in all different directions. We leftovers stare off dejectedly into space like a club of school-dance rejects, a feeling I know all too much about. I watch my busy and not-so-busy classmates and try to keep my eyes off Leslie. She has her back to me, working away at a clunky computer that sounds like it's lifting something heavy every time she opens a file.

School is like a zoo. Peace Train attempts a long bomb from his computer by the printer. His receiver, Lounge Lizard, who's scoping Leslie's rack, gets a ball of paper in the cornea. It glances off him and rolls in a loop around the legs of my desk, coming to a rest against my shoelaces.

Ms. Wessin made a big mistake bringing us to the computer lab—Bubble Butt talks with some pervert in a chat room; Curious George downloads porn.

I pick the crumpled note off the floor and read:

Rick (really Dick)—
Did You hear about Millie's f'ing head?
HolY s!
Teachers ain't talking.
Probably that Kirt Moore guY = fag!
You think, Homes?
Wessin'd be hot if she wore sandals!

So much for my work going unnoticed. A needling pain stabs my chest, like a sculptor is aiming his chisel right at the bridge of my rib cage and tapping with his hammer.

"Arty?"

Leslie looks over her shoulder, hair bouncing like rapids down her back—the way it was last night. She hits the *A* button on her keyboard every so often to make it sound like she's typing. Growing bored, she pushes back in her wheeled chair and rolls away from her desk toward me. She crosses the border onto my desk, where I can really smell her Octane blasting.

"What?" I say.

"I want to meet him."

"Who?" I know damn well who she is talking about.

"The boy in the leather jacket you're always talking to. The boss. The one who sent you over to school last night."

"Jack?" I say. Last night. Last night.

"His name's Jack?" she says, making a note in her Palm Pilot.

"Yeah."

She forms legs with the index and middle fingers of her left hand and "strolls" up the back of my neck. "Bring him to my house tonight, seven o'clock," she says.

"What for?" I say.

"I want to meet him," she says, shrugging. "I want

to know what he's like." I could tell her all about him, all the juicy dirt. After all, she did help me clean up last night when we needed to cover my mess. She's in it now, too. Isn't that what she wants out of life, to be *in* everything?

I don't know what I was thinking last night. I felt like someone else, like I held a loaded gun; like Kerouac probably feels when he tries to solve everyone's problems. Powerful. If Leslie wants to meet him, then I'm going to let her find out firsthand what that means.

"Arty?"

I don't look at her. I wish I were back where I was before all of this happened. I wish I couldn't talk to girls again.

When the bell rings, I grab my backpack off the desk and my booster seat off the chair and then hurry out of the lab before Leslie even has a chance to stand.

I spend my lunch period avoiding anyone with a red pin. But I can feel them tailing me, scoping the scrapes on my face as they swish by in the doorways. I see a glimmer of something in their eyes as they look at me, a shine I've never picked up on before—something that might be respect. I don't want respect.

I sit at the farthest, emptiest table in the cafeteria next to Kid with No Legs and Albino Girl. None of us talk, but when Albino Girl asks for an extra napkin, I hand it to her without hesitation. She wipes the boy's face and talks quietly to him like a good mother might. At one point Leslie enters, scanning the room, and I duck low so she doesn't see me.

It's weird, because I've wasted the last few years of my life sitting alone in my tower wishing to be around other people. All I want is to walk to school every day without being bothered. To go to the movies and not be afraid of the dark. Life is not easy for me. Unlike everyone else, I have to *try* to survive. I have to inject drugs every day, into my thighs, into my stomach, and it hurts sometimes. It hurts a lot. But I keep doing it.

It's like that gerbil in its wheel and Mom on her bike. Like Grampa hacking away endlessly in those old coal mines, or blasting away in the quarry. Look what digging forever did to him. Not a damn thing. Nothing ever changes for the better.

Fifty years down the line, I'll probably still be at war with my stupid, pizza-faced gorilla twin brother. That is where I'm going—nowhere.

I crumple my lunch sack and stand to leave.

"I like your necklace," Albino Girl says. She points at my throat, where Mom's gift swings on its metal cord. The red jewel stays bright, even in the dim cafeteria light.

"Thanks," I say. "I made it."

"Nice," she says, and gives me a thumbs-up.

"Have a good one," Kid with No Legs says to me,

and he wrestles his hand into a deformed thumbs-up to match the girl's. I don't think I've ever heard his voice before. It's sort of breathless, like the stopping gasp of an air conditioner.

"You, too," I say. Albino Girl rubs the boy's knobby back and looks deep into his eyes, even though he doesn't seem to notice.

On my way to biology, I'm blocked by this mess of kids that clogs the lobby and throws the rest of the hallway traffic into gridlock. Kids shuffle single file toward a collection of folding tables near the trophy case. A draped banner quivers in the breeze of the front doors as people duck in and out for lunch. Our school cop reclines on a staircase, paging through a guitar magazine with greasy potato-chip fingers.

I cut in on the closest line to scout the situation, maneuvering around bodies, and before I know it, I'm near the head of the line.

"Would you like to sign the schoolwide pledge not to drink alcohol up until and during the summer vacation?" Rose Purdy says cheerfully. She sits across the table from me, talking over a mountain of pledge forms. Girls in white paper hats sit on either side of her, recording names on clipboards and handing out buttons that say: *It's Fly to Stay Dry*.

"What are you doing here?" I say.

"I'm on the Summer Pledge committee," she says.

Summer Pledge? What is she talking about? "I thought you only had to be on the dance committee," I say. "Do you have to help with this 'cause you're still in trouble or something?"

Rose lowers her head and squeezes her fingers into solid sledgehammer fists. Even when she's sitting, she's taller than I am, like Wonder Woman with a mean streak. "Just sign the oath," she says through clenched teeth.

"What for?" I say. "I don't drink."

"All the more reason to sign it, all right?" she says, whacking my knuckles with the pen.

"Okay, fine." I scrawl my signature across the dotted line.

"It doesn't really matter what the event is," she says, not making eye contact. "Our people are always out hunting for opportunities, and it's my job to make sure all festivities serve our greater organizational purposes. The war goes on, Arty." Then she grins ear to ear.

"Congratulations!" she shouts, sitting up in her chair. "I'm proud of you, kiddo." Even though she's gesturing to the pen, and my signature, and the fine print of Summer Pledge restrictions, I know that she's really talking about the letter, the head in the locker, phase two—and that her smile is real.

"Hey, Betsy!" Rose calls to the girl on her left. "Hand me some more of those buttons, will you?"

"Sure, Kim," the girl says, resisting the temptation

to cop a glance at my smallness and handing over a transparent plastic tube filled with buttons.

"Kim?" I say.

Rose unhooks the pin from the back of a button and jabs at me, and I have to dodge to keep from being impaled. "What's in a name?" she says. "And here's a little advice: Try to enjoy my good moods when you can. They're hard to come by."

I take the pin and fix it to the front of my shirt, nodding to show I understand.

"Consider that a Purple Heart," Rose says.

Then, leaning around me, she flicks an index finger at the next guy in line. "You," she says. The dude jolts like he just got a Summer Pledge pin jabbed in his butt cheek, and he stumbles up to the table just in time for: "Would you like to sign the schoolwide pledge not to drink alcohol up until and during the summer vacation?"

The guy, who I've never seen before, drops his jaw to answer, but as his first words exit, an excited shout drowns out his voice.

"Stop him, Dennis!" someone screams. At first I think it's a girl, a glass-shattering shriek. But hobbling down the hall on a crooked knee comes our school principal, his face rearranged with fury.

Kurt sprints ahead of him, aiming for the front doors. He hurls his six-foot-three frame toward the parking lot in long primal bounds that I can only dream about. The school cop—aka Dennis—reacts like he's on expired batteries and rises to his feet, spilling his lunch all over the floor in front of him. Then, as he jukes to the right, his very own puddle of spreading V8 juice slips him backward, his arms whirling.

Kurt blows through the doors, banging his elbow on the doorframe, which makes him screech, trip, and grab his arm.

Still, he's free. He turns to make sure he really made it, eyes wide with disbelief. His cheeks shine with wetness.

He sees me.

Separated by the sheets of smudgy glass, we get a good look at each other.

I see no resemblance.

SOUTHWORTH COMFORT

At first the cops looked for me. They wanted to ask me questions. But apparently Principal Malone, along with a gaggle of insistent teachers, told them I am a "good boy."

Suckers.

Kerouac and I walk up to Pinewood Terrace at about seven, but not exactly. Kerouac has been sitting on a bench underneath a fancy lamppost for the past several minutes, flipping through a blue binder with Leslie's name stamped on its spine. After one particularly messy page, he grunts and lets the smoke in his mouth leak out the sides.

"Whoever put this together did a great job," he says. "Remind me to bring it up at the next meeting."

It had been easy convincing him to come. When I mentioned Leslie's name, he flipped off the switch on the jigsaw he was operating and lowered his goggles around his neck. He gave me a quizzical look as the blade came to a scraping stop. "I've been waiting for this," he had said. "Nice work, Arty-man. Really nice. Dermott's got clout, or will when the time comes."

I don't know what he means, and frankly, I don't care. Life is screwed up that way, and I feel nothing. I should be happy, but I'm not. Even the anger is gone; I had kind of grown to rely on that, but it left me, too. I've got nothing now.

I stand on the corner of two streets called Perfection Place and Heavenly Lane, where a small octagonal sign shows a tiny graphic of a pooping dog with a red slash through it. In all my visits to Leslie's place, I have never seen a single one of her neighbors. Sprinklers spring up from the dirt at six in the morning and seven in the evening, machine-gunning the eerily green grass like clockwork and then slipping back underground again. Men come for the trash. Men deliver groceries. Men manicure the lawns. They drop things off and pick things up. But no human face ever gazes out from an inside window. No shirtless men walk around with a beer in one hand and a flyswatter in the other, like men do in my neighborhood.

The people of Pinewood Terrace will probably roll

out of here in those garbage trucks when they die, a funeral procession led by an escort of illegal gardeners and digital–cable installation specialists. They will have moved in, lived their lives, and then been carted out again without anyone beyond the development walls ever noticing. Nothing about this place seems as perfect or heavenly as it probably should.

Kerouac finishes up and flicks his cigarette into a flower bed. He turns toward Leslie's block and starts to walk, hands in his pockets, blue binder clamped under an arm. I hurry to keep up.

As we cross the street, Camilla strolls out of Leslie's driveway and turns down our stretch of sidewalk. She looks as good as always, that long ponytail slithering around her neck and hanging down her front like some kind of leash, and she wears that stupid blue maid outfit with the frills and the collar. I steal a glance at her amazing eyes, and she looks back at me only for a second. Then, I swear, I see her and Kerouac exchange looks, and maybe even a nod.

Or it could just be my imagination.

Camilla left the door to Leslie's house open.

Kerouac lifts his nose like a dog and sniffs the air. The long hallway ripples with invisible incense, and is lit only by candles in holders on a wall. Their flames cast watery golden shadows along the marble floor.

I lead him down the hallway, past the two studies,

the atrium, the exercise room, and the art studio, then along the gallery to the home theater and the bar.

Leslie sits at the counter with her white legs folded and smooth—an ice sculpture in jean shorts. Her hair is swept up into a sculpted bun and harpooned with what look like chopsticks. Because I know her, I know that those diamonds in her ears are the real thing.

"Would you like something to drink?" she says. Her eyes track Kerouac as he approaches a stool. He decides against sitting and stands, resting his weight against the bar. If she had a tip jar, he'd probably drop a twenty and make a pass at her. His grin shows his yellow smoker's teeth.

"What do you have back there?" he says.

"What do you want?"

"What have you got?"

"Everything. We've got everything," she says. I can tell she's eager to please.

"You don't got what I want. I bet you," Kerouac says.

"We have everything," she says.

Kerouac drags a hand along the shiny buffed wood. It gleams like a brand-new bowling lane. "Whiskey on the rocks then," he says.

"Straight?"

"You heard what I said," Kerouac says. He plops down on one of the stools and makes himself at home, casually sifting through the bowl of bar mix looking for the peanuts. I sit next to him, having to climb the stool like a ladder to reach the cushion.

Leslie fumbles around the bar for a minute, reading bottles, clanking corkscrews, sliding drawers, and holding labels up to the light. Kerouac watches closely, his bloodshot eyes staring and unblinking over bags of sleep deprivation. I wonder what he thinks as he drums his fingers up and down the bar, leaving foggy gray fingerprints. Is this just one of a hundred house calls?

Leslie finds the right bottle and fills a short glass with ice cubes and whiskey and then hands it to Kerouac. He raises it in what might be a toast and then inhales the contents in a vacuum suck.

"We saw your maid," he says, slurping liquid from around his lips. He holds out his pack of Camels. At first Leslie seems stumped by the offer. But she bounces back, rolling her eyes like a snob and tugging a smoke from the foil wrapper.

"Where was she going?" I say, because I really want to know.

"I gave her the night off," Leslie says.

"Gutsy," Kerouac says. "Can you make it without her? I give you twenty-four hours."

"I've seen you in school," Leslie says, ignoring his sarcasm. She holds the cigarette between her thumb and index finger, and it's obvious that she's never held one in her life. Kerouac leans over and lights its tip.

"I'm hard to miss," he says.

"Well, then, why don't you tell me about yourself," Leslie says. "How long have you lived in Southworth? Do you like it here?"

"Is this an interrogation?" he says.

"Of course not," she says. She taps her cigarette and misses the brass ashtray by a mile.

"Well, I was born here, raised here, and I'm still here," Kerouac says. He spins in a complete circle on his stool. "Anything else you wanna know?" He spins. "Yeah, my parents are still together. No, none of my sisters are drug addicts or felons." He spins. "Pop ain't a drunk. Mom's got no men on the side." He spins. "I can't complain, really. Oh, once, I burned my thigh with a lit cigarette when I got yelled at by a teacher, but mostly to get attention." He stops spinning. His smile never wavers. "That's the best I got. Never tried to hang myself, blow my brains out, or chop the old wrists off—nothing like that."

He takes a drag off his smoke. "So that's that; case closed. Hope I don't disappoint. How about you?" He extends a skeletal arm and grazes her knuckles. She reacts, snapping her hand back against her chest. "All I know about you are a bunch of nicknames and one dumb joke. What else you got?" His teeth clamp down on the Camel filter and I hear the paper crunch.

Leslie does not respond. Instead, she tops off his whiskey and whips up a pitcher of frozen margaritas. And they drink.

And we all drink.

I've never consumed an ounce of alcohol in my life, but I know it flows in my veins, courtesy of Dad, thank you very much. I drink Leslie's margaritas. A sour limey flavor sticks to my tongue. Each sip makes my throat burn, so I take it slow, nursing a single icy glass and staying quiet.

I watch Leslie and Kerouac try to outmaneuver each other. Before I know it I've forgotten where I am. The life-size Chewbacca bares his teeth at me. Lightbulbs resemble science textbook supernovas. I take my sweatshirt off. I spin on my stool. The music sounds like underwater music. I eat the bar nuts just because they're there. I consider taking off my shirt but don't. I spin on my stool some more. This is nice. It makes things easy to forget.

Leslie matches Kerouac drink for drink and cigarette for cigarette. Don't know how many. The room disappears under this bank of smog. Only the neon St. Pauli Girl cuts through the weather, like a bright and busty beacon. The same ten songs play over in stereo loops.

Chewbacca stands in the corner by the aquarium, drenched in darkness.

I lose track of what we talk about. Leslie and Kerouac don't seem to be keeping track, either, 'cause we've moved to the carpet and now sit in a triangle with our legs out in front of us, talking about the cartoons we remember from when we were kids. Leslie's deteriorating bartender's aim leaves wet outlines around our glasses.

Her face shines in the blue St. Pauli neon, but not in a good way. The loose hair around her ears hangs tangled; sweaty, stringy, clumps of it pasted to her cheeks and neck. Everything out of her mouth sounds mushy at the end and the beginning. She drinks before she even stops talking now, and her voice bubbles in the tumbler.

At one point Kerouac excuses himself to the bathroom and sways down the narrow corridor like he's walking the deck of a rolling ship. He leaves so suddenly that Leslie and I sit suspended in total silence.

We search the bottoms of our drinks for something to say as the tequila burns in my guts. It feels like acid eating through my pipes. Leslie won't even look at me, and the more I feel her fighting it, the hotter my stomach cooks. She is about to get up. I know she is.

"Why did you do that to me?" I say.

"What?" she says. She sounds annoyed.

"Parade me around in that stupid egg suit, that's what. Why?"

"I didn't do anything," she says.

"You could have just told me about the costumes,"

I say. "I would have worn the eggshell. I would have worn anything you asked me to. But you didn't ask. So you made me look stupid. And I don't need any help with that, you know?"

She takes a long swig. "I thought you wanted the attention," she says. "Isn't that what we were doing?"

"I never wanted attention," I say. "Only you did."

"We both did," she says, glaring.

"I only wanted *your* attention," I say. "And after all that time we spent together, you never once asked me why the hell I'm so small." My buzz trips my words, knocking them fumbling from my lips.

"I thought you don't like it when people ask," she says, and jabs a finger in my chest. "You always say you hate it."

"Strangers," I say. "But we're friends."

With trembling fingers she takes a cigarette and tries to light it, but her match keeps missing the tip. I take her wrist and guide the flame. "It doesn't matter why I am different," I say, "only that I am."

She shifts her jaw back and forth, avoiding my gaze. The bones click. "So what's wrong with you, then?" she says. "What's the big damn deal?"

I can't. Too little, too late. I turn, inhaling, face pinching into an involuntary frown. I look at the St. Pauli Girl, the light in the smoke. I wait for Kerouac to take me home.

When he returns from the bathroom, humming some rap song and zipping his fly, Leslie lurches over, rubbing her half-open eyes and grabs his arm. "I want to join," she says.

"Join what?" Kerouac says.

"Your group, the gang, whatever," she says. "I want in."

"I heard you gave a hand last night," he says. He takes a cherry from a bowl on the counter and drops it in her glass. "You showed real heart, real initiative."

"Thanks," she says. "It was a rush."

"I'll bet it was," he says. "But sorry, you're not welcome."

The sharp edge in his voice lingers, even over the music. And at that moment, the CD changer hiccups in the cabinet and rotates with a hiss. Leslie's face toughens, the muscles rigid and wrinkled, almost like it's aging through time-lapse photography. Her hair shines a shade of gray under the cloudy bar lights.

"Why not?" she says.

"Because you're not," Kerouac says. "To join you have to want to help people. And you don't want to help anyone but yourself, and that's the way it's always gonna be. I know you. I know your type."

It's funny. I see her swing a split second before she tries it. The fist misses Kerouac, who flattens up against the counter as if he knew this was coming. Then

Leslie's balance fails her. Wobbling away from the bar, she snaps out and clenches a handful of Chewbacca's back hair to keep from toppling. Her lips part in surprise, like she's about to blow on some hot soup, but then I catch that old honor student flash in her green eyes. Her lips change, curling into a snarl.

She flicks her cigarette at Kerouac before hitting the floor. When she lands she springs right back up again, swiping with French-manicured fingernails. She kicks and spits. Her shouts ring off the white walls.

"You think you can come in here and tell me what I can and can't do! Who the hell do you—?" But before she can finish the insult, she tips to one side again and clutches the bar with one hand, the alcohol taking effect. A rubbery leg knocks the nearly empty pitcher of margaritas across the carpet. The room fills with the scent of sour limes.

At last gravity sucks her to the floor again with a bang. I watch her hair come free and unfurl along the carpet to the nearby hallway marble. The little chopsticks clatter and roll. Leslie lies on her side, growling, her jean shorts soaking up the spreading yellow margarita puddle.

Kerouac wipes his mouth and flicks his glass across the counter. "My work is done here," he says. "And don't forget, kids. There's a party at the quarry on Sunday if you're interested. Everyone's invited to that." He drops the stub of his Camel into the bar ash-tray and then rinses his hands in the sink. "Even you, baby," he says to the squirming Leslie.

He leaves the door wide open on his way out.

I crouch down next to her, avoiding the mess. "Leslie?" I say. "Are you okay?"

She doesn't look at me, and stands up doubled over, wrapping her hair around her face. Dragging her feet, she moves across the room to that freaky meat locker door, which makes a suction-cup sound as it unlocks. She doesn't speak, and slips behind the silver door, fading into the foul-smelling fog.

I grope after her, I don't know why, into the stink of eyes and cadavers, rubber gloves and metal instruments.

Something warm wraps around my waist. An arm. Lips tremble close to my ear. "Arty," she whispers, and I feel her full chest press against mine, as she shakes, so freezing, scary freezing, even under her skintight sweater. A sweet breath seeps down my collar. My toes curl.

But even with all her padding, that softness I used to dream about, Leslie feels hard to me.

She struggles as I pry her fingers from my sleeve, one by one. "I'm sorry," I say, and step away. I never meant to hurt her, but I need out of here. No matter how hard I try, I'm not going to be able to get her dead, cold smells off me.

Near the door I feel her hand close around my shoe. She is invisible in the mist. "Can I keep the list, the good things?" she says.

"Sure," I say. "Sure." And I walk out the door.

Kerouac's words ring in my ears, like in a deserted warehouse. An echo.

"You can't save everybody." "You can't save everybody." "You can't save everybody."

AGAINST THE ROPES

THE SCHOOL NEWSLETTER OF
THE FILLMORE HIGH SCHOOL BOXING TURTLES

"A turtle only makes progress when it sticks out its neck."
—Anonymous

WEEK OF JUNE 6–12 (LAST WEEK OF SCHOOL!)

 Sign the Summer Pledge and do the right thing this vacation, brought to you by the Upstanding Historical Girls and Pioneer Homemakers Association. You won't be sorry! "Free" Summer Pledge T-shirts cost $12 at sign-up tables in the lobby. *Summer Pledge: Do it for you; do it for them; do it for us.* (*Summer Pledge* is a trademark of the Upstanding Historical Girls and Pioneer Homemakers Association.)

 Need a little mental exercise over the summer? Ms. Wessin can help get your brain into shape. E-mail her today to discuss what you're bad at: kwessin @globenet.org.

🐢 Come see Shakespeare's sort of classic musical *Some Merry Guys of Windsor* this summer, starring Leslie Dermott and Vincent Nguyen. See it as the Bard intended—on the fifty-yard line!

🐢 **NEW:** Southworth Crew, Sunday mornings at 7:00 at the reservoir. Call Leslie: 579-9877.

🐢 **NEW:** Future Entrepreneurs of America Club, Tuesdays at 5:00 in the library. Call Leslie: 579-9877.

🐢 He is out there, plotting against our cherished school! You know who we're talking about. Keep your turtle eyes open for the traitor among us.

MiNiNG THE QUARRY

It's Sunday night, and I sit in the lowered scoop of a chipped and rusty old bulldozer, missing my grampa. I came here to the quarry before the party to watch the sun set above the high cliff walls. Now the darkness makes it so I can't see where the cliff edge stops and the drop into nothing begins.

Scooting to the front of the scoop, I look down on hundreds of parked cars, their headlights mingling and projecting a circular halo of yellow light onto the quarry floor. It looks like a UFO warming up for liftoff. Students dance, collide, and fling themselves into one another. They link arms and fly apart, all to the music of a student rock band called Atomic Suppository. Its members wear the letter *A* painted across their chests in a red, killing floor color. In the center of the activity rests Millie's obliterated remains, decked out with candles and class pictures like some sacred shrine.

Members of Affront line the cliffs above, peering down on the collective bump-and-grind in the canyon. They sit in quiet clusters playing cards and smoking. White Christmas lights droop from the huge lumps of abandoned mine equipment that collect dust along the cliffs. Gus Van Mussberger plucks an acoustic guitar from his seat at the operator's wheel of a fossilized crane. When his fingernails click on them, the strings sound like the comforting chimes of one of those old grandfather clocks. He leans back, grinning, wearing worn cutoffs like a hash-puffing Huck Finn, his bare feet up on the steering wheel. Occasionally, Gus sings a few notes in a clear, surprisingly gentle voice. I don't know the words, but the tune sounds nice to me, anyway.

I should be celebrating with my classmates, but as usual I stand apart from the party. I don't know why I came, really; maybe to watch everyone else think about the future. Because down in the quarry below, the students of Fillmore High rock like their world will end at the stroke of midnight.

They see this last week of school as a time of promise. I do not. They have a strange faith that summer vacation will change things for the better. I do not. They suck down truckloads of beer, hoping that high school will all be part of the past soon enough. I do not.

I once thought things could change, too.

I stretch out alone in my chipped yellow scoop and watch the rising bonfire smoke. Because I don't want to stumble drunk into the future quite yet, I'd rather things just go back to how they used to be. I don't want a future if this is how I get it. I'm sick of looking across the gates of Pinewood Terrace to find the greener grass.

Kerouac stands by himself to my right, at the very tip of a narrow ledge of rock. It gives me goose bumps to see him swaying so close to the cliff. He drags on a cigarette and sprinkles ash out into the air like he's adding magic spices to a cauldron, all the while seeming to contemplate the implications of the drop.

He wears leather pants, and a red flannel shirt that flaps in the breeze. The way he hunches over makes him look a bit like my grampa, how the old guy used to stoop in his stained and cigar-blotched button-down flannel and point out the mouths of long-forgotten mine shafts. Watching Kerouac's shirt flutter, I almost expect to hear Grampa's voice telling weird quarry stories. Like the day Mer Steinmetz lost his foot under a train car. Or the time Spud Mutland barfed blood into a bucket.

I miss Grampa more than ever tonight.

He was someone who gave a damn, no matter

what. There are very few people like that, who see all the things about you, every screw-up and bad call, and still find a reason to like you, even *love* you. Those folks never give up on you. They always see the best, even when you can't. It's like that time Mom said, "I'll always love you," and she was, like, deadly serious.

Grampa actually did that, too. He was my "always" guy. You count on guys like him. He was so damn cool.

And now he's always dead.

Always pretty much sucks when you think about it that way.

Man, I am in total dumpsville. I listen to the sound of my breathing mixed with the boom of the band below, and the soft, almost babyish cooing of Gus and his guitar.

Then I notice Kerouac looking right at me, a frown on his wasted face. He walks slowly over to my bull-dozer and then crawls into the scoop beside me, extending those long leather-wrapped legs out over the dirt.

"Great view, huh?" he says.

I nod, but I don't feel like talking.

"So tell me," he says, "how's your first taste of freedom?"

I still don't feel like talking. He thinks I'm relaxing here, savoring a victory. What he doesn't know is that I'm not thinking about Kurt at all. I think about Grampa and how good that view was from atop his motorized shopping cart. I want to feel that good again.

"Yup," Kerouac says, as if he thinks he's reading my mind. "Revenge can be sweet."

In the quarry Atomic Suppository's current song breaks down into stray guitar twangs and a shimmering cymbal, and the lead singer thanks the audience with a string of inventive cusswords. Up here the sounds are more like an echo of the real world reaching us from far away. Up here Gus floats his gentle lyrics like he's blowing bubbles or casting spells.

"Don't feel too bad," Kerouac says, patting me on the knee. "You did what you had to do." But I don't know which one of us he's talking about. Do people *have* to do anything?

"You know, I've been thinking about nominating you for a position near the top, Arty-man. A little more responsibility, maybe. This organization has a lot of room for advancement, and you have an extreme streak that I dig, man. Really. You don't know where to draw the line. Hell, I don't think you even *know* about the line. Those are the kind of people we're looking for."

I try to squeeze Kerouac out of my mind. During the past month he has become more of a person than a nickname, and tonight my brain feels too overcrowded for him to slip inside and screw around.

Reaching under my shirt, I pull out the pendant that I made for Grampa, the one he never got around to opening when he was alive. It seems to weigh heavier on my palm than it did against my chest. I had almost completely forgotten about it. The fake jewel in the center of the knob twinkles under the Christmas bulbs. I turn the pendant over in my hands, letting all the tiny crystal fissures catch the light.

"That's nice," Kerouac says. "Family heirloom?"

I nod.

I look closer. The workmanship is better than I would have expected from myself. I'm not a patient person, but these intricately carved lines have been well brushed and polished, and the red crystal seems to have been recut where it had once chipped. All of these things require oodles of patience. When I think harder, I can't remember finding this knob at all, with its tiny sculpted leaves curling out from the corners. It looks like one of my creations, but in the details it isn't.

Then I see the inscription.

It faces me from between my middle and index fingers, two letters side by side: *KM*.

Kurt Moore. I have to squint in the semidarkness, but there's no mistake.

Kurt made this. It had been *his* gift to Grampa, not mine.

Turning the knob over and over in my hands, I really think about my twin brother. Not about what I think of him, or what he must think of me, but just about this gorilla of a guy named Kurt.

The name alone means nothing. When we were little kids, my name for him was Curry, like the spice, and his name for me, according to Mom, was some scary noise, like Aiieeee, that sounded like a chick in a horror movie right before she's hacked up and gets her pieces flushed down the commode.

Mom always called him Kurtis. Still does sometimes when she's probing him for the rare straight answer. Grampa called him Kurtis, too, but in a nice, grown-up way, like they were two good old boys having coffee in a booth at Denny's.

This gets me thinking about Grampa, and Kurt, and me. I guess Kurt had been there the whole time, collecting trash with us at the old plant and making presents to give to Mom. We worked on them together sometimes, too; at least I think we did. He was with me that day in the grocery store, when Grampa started his long, painful trip to the grave right there on the checkerboard tile of aisle seven.

I wouldn't even be surprised if Kurt misses Grampa almost as much as I do.

I remember the day when Kurt and I found Dad's good-bye note, which was more of a threat than a farewell. *Don't follow me,* it said on the outside of the folded paper, but I don't think we needed any convincing. We stared at the note on the kitchen table like we were playing Russian roulette and that folded calendar page was the loaded gun. Neither of us would touch it. But after a long time, Kurt was the one who finally reached out and unfolded the paper and read.

Kurt's been with me all along.

Behind me gravel crunches and tires spin. I lean around the bulldozer scoop to see a vintage Volkswagen Beetle tearing along a high canyon road, its high beams bouncing. Kerouac grins, then claps the crud from his hands and jumps up, pulling me to my feet next to him. A mixed cloud of dust and exhaust travels toward us along the outline of the quarry, with the car out in front like it's being chased.

We back away as the Beetle slides to a stop dangerously close to the cliffs. The door swings open, and out steps Rose Purdy, dressed in a lime green sundress that shows off her long, recently shaved legs. Her knees and shins are polka-dotted with small round Band-Aids. On her face a chalky crust of makeup replaces her usual streaks of grease, and even though she looks sort of like a zombie hooker, I have to admit she cleans up pretty well. The Beetle's headlights give her figure a thin silver outline.

"You look like crap," she says to me.

Looking her up and down, Kerouac moseys over to give Rose a kiss on the forehead. Then he lights a cigarette for each of them and hands hers over. Together they slouch against the VW with their hands on each other's hips, faces glowing orange like their freak love is warming them from the inside out.

Rose looks back at me. "Seriously," she asks Kerouac, "is he okay?"

"He's fine," Kerouac says.

The knob-pendant feels like a whole chest of drawers hanging around my neck. Rose glances at me again from around Kerouac's pale skull. Their fingers intertwine, and I notice how hers aren't stained yet from cigarettes, not like Kerouac's browned sausage-link fingers.

I squeeze the cold knob and then turn to head back toward my little rodent den inside the bulldozer scoop, where I can be alone, where I can think about the future.

Then Rose speaks, and her words pop out like she's coughing up food. "The cops are chasing your brother, Arty," she blurts. The second he hears this, Kerouac shoots her a look, and not a nice one. He grinds his cigarette between his stained teeth.

"What?" I say, and stop in the dust.

"It's under control," Kerouac says a second later. "No worries."

"Is it?" Rose says. "Paul up at Viking reported that Kurt called in for takeout ten minutes ago." As the words jump out, Rose begins to sound more panicked and lets go of Kerouac's hand.

"Everyone received that intelligence," Kerouac says. "And like I said, it's all under control." A cell phone in his pants pocket rings with a techno beat, but he ignores it and keeps up the confident smile.

"What's going on?" I say.

"I don't know what to tell you, all right?" Rose says. "We have some reports coming in. We think Kurt's skipping town."

I turn to the one person who always seems to be in control. "Jack?" I say. "Tell me what's happening."

As soon as I use his first name, Kerouac turns away. He concentrates on his every deep inhalation like that cigarette is his oxygen tank. Down in the quarry, Atomic Suppository launches into a new "tune," louder than anything in its first set, a sound like a lumber mill exploding.

"You wanted him gone, didn't you?" Kerouac says.

"I think," I say, and the words sound pathetic even to me.

"You *think*?" he says. "Thinking doesn't get you anywhere. What do you *want*, Arty?"

"I don't know what I want," I say, and for a few seconds, a kind of anger stirs up in me that I've never felt before. It feels like my body can't hold it all, like I'm going to break into pieces just like good old Millie.

"Think about this, then," Kerouac says, pointing his cigarette at me. "Kurt didn't do it. Millie. He didn't do it." His dark, almost black eyes meet mine in a cold stare, and it scares me to death.

Kerouac knows.

He knows that I was starting to believe that Kurt really had kidnapped Millie and lynched her from that construction crane. He knows that I have been making a list of all the ways Kurt could have done it, just to convince myself that he was as bad as I thought, as bad as I want him to be.

There is a loud clunking sound as Gus steps down from his seat in the cage of the crane and lurches over. Cocking his head like a dog, he taps Kerouac on the back of his red flannel shirt. It's impossible to see the wheels turning in Gus's head because he has no wheels there to turn. But even he understands some things.

"Kurt didn't do it?" he says.

Kerouac smiles weakly and wipes the gathered dirt off Gus's shoulders. "Yeah, Gus-man. He didn't do a damn thing."

"But the cops," Gus says.

"He'll be fine," Kerouac says. "I've already taken care of everything in case this happened: a hideout, an alibi, fake IDs—the guy is set. When he needs us, we'll be there." He takes Rose's hand again, and she looks at him with something more than love, his slick bald scalp reflecting all the prickly stars of those Christmas lights.

"What do you mean you'll be there?" I say.

"What do you think, Arty?" Kerouac says, and for once he seems a bit ticked off. "I told you that I help people. I don't pick and choose. I give help where it's needed." He stands up straight and raises his head, and right then I know he's bought into his own pitch line, his own stinking BS.

"He's right," Rose says. She's not leaning my way anymore, as if she ever was; she stands by her man, just like a good woman is supposed to do, even if he's a punk, or a crook, or a liar. "Everybody needs help sometimes."

I look at Kerouac, then at Rose, and then lastly at Gus, who seems to have even less of a clue as to what's going on than I do, which is no clue at all. I can almost feel the growth hormone boiling in my veins, and I want to scream my little head off. "So first you help me, and then you help Kurt?" I say. "What kind of messed-up help is that?" Swinging one leg wildly, I kick the rusty front bumper of Rose's Beetle. It feels like someone just blasted off my big toe with a shotgun, so much so that I have to lift the injured foot up off the ground and lean on the hood of the car.

"Careful," Rose says. "That's vintage."

"Who cares?" I scream, my voice cracking.

I sit my itty-bitty body down on the bumper and hang my midget head. Where is Grampa now? Where is my mom when I need her? I finger the pendant under the collar of my shirt, touching the sharp corners and smooth surfaces. I want to make everything new again, like this scuzzy old chest-of-drawers doorknob. To fix my life so it's better than it was before. I tried to do it one way, but I made a mess of everything.

Kerouac leaves Rose to come and watch over me; I can smell his strange Kerouac odor, a mixture of cigarette smoke and chemical lemon. "I think you missed what I was trying to show you," he says. He puts one spidery hand on my head and gives it a shake. "Everybody is a bully to somebody, Arty-man." Then he points his burning cigarette toward me. "Even us."

I think of my twin brother and me scrounging in the trash, looking for gold in all that garbage.

My hand makes a fist, and I turn away from the suffocating energy of Atomic Suppository, and the swirling fireflies of burning ash rising up from the quarry floor. I stare down at the ground where the tire marks of Rose's Beetle form a straight track backward along the twisting dirt road into the darkness. It is a perfect, unalterable path, and I know I must follow it.

So I run, limping down the road, leaving Affront's members scattered along those far cliffs, where they gaze down on the world below as if from a poor white-trash Mount Olympus. I step into the Beetle's clear tracks and work back through the dust, but I don't get far because I think I broke my toe with that moronic kick.

No matter. A hand grips my collar and snaps me up into the air, catapulting me softly onto a saddle of broad, sweaty shoulders. The faint fragrance of pot and Old Spice clings to a frighteningly wide neck that can only belong to Gus Van Mussberger.

He marches us back to the lights of the party and makes a beeline for the driver's-side door of the Beetle. Firecrackers pitter-patter like Bubble Wrap popping down deep in the quarry, and the student body roars with approval.

"Get in," Gus says, opening the car door. "I'm jacking this sucker."

He has the plastic cover off the steering column before I can fasten my seat belt and then holds the wires up to the interior light and bites off their insulated ends. The stripped copper sparks once, twice, thrice.

Sighing, Rose ducks her head in the window and pushes Gus away from the ignition. "Use my keys, you idiot," she says.

Then she turns to me, cigarette skewed, face reflected in the side-view mirror. "Look in the backseat when you get the chance, all right?" she says. "But I didn't tell you to. I never said a word."

"What is it?" I say. She doesn't respond, but pulls back out of the window and reattaches herself to Kerouac's hip.

Gus revs the engine and makes the sign of the devil with pinkie and index fingers raised in fleshy horns.

"Let's do it," I say.

"Always" guy to the freaking rescue.

WELCOME TO THE MONKEY HOUSE

Gus swings the Beetle around a corner, narrowly missing a park bench and the kissing couple seated on it.

He is more alive than I've ever seen him. He lowers his window and bellows into the trees as they blur by. With one hand on the wheel, he uses the other to punch buttons on the radio, only to settle on a metal station that sounds like an express train broadsiding a silverware shop.

We tear up Millard Fillmore Avenue heading north, swerving around slower cars, most of which are actually driving well over the speed limit. The school flashes past as if it's a hallucination of fluorescent lamps and flagpoles, a bad memory I'll have to revisit come tomorrow morning.

Remembering Rose's last words, I unbuckle my belt and wiggle around to check the backseat. A cardboard file box sits wedged in the floor behind Gus, and I snag it and pull it up into my lap. As I lift, a small collection of papers falls from where it had been resting on top of the box, and flies apart in a flurry of loose pages. I snatch them one by one and try to put them back in order.

They look very familiar—the font, the format, the photographs—and then I catch the name KURT MOORE stamped boldly across the top margins.

The mysterious section C of Kurt's secret red binder.

I flip through the pages and scan each sheet from top to bottom as Gus glances over curiously, oblivious to my discovery. In my hot little hands, I hold practice tests that have been pulled from trash cans, the paper still stiff with soda stains and black with coffee grounds. There are tutoring schedules, complicated school transcripts, a couple of handwritten notes from Mom dotted with purple ballpoint hearts, and even a number of assignment slips bearing the recognizable signature of one Ms. Karen Wessin.

Last but not least, I unfold a long, colorful brochure for Mount Kennedy Military School, "the reformatory miracle that you and your family have been praying for."

So what does this mean? That Kurt has been cramming for military school? *My* Kurt? In the light of the passing streetlights I look at the brochure for Mount

Kennedy again, straining my eyes. There's a picture of a campus, a bell tower, and kids mingling on a set of sun-baked steps. It doesn't make sense. None of these Mount Kennedy idiots look at all like Kurt. They look normal, almost grown-up, and their uniforms are covered with medals and crap like that.

So he's been working this whole time? My brain fights against this truth. Kurt and Mom and Ms. Wessin, they've been having some kind of superstudy orgy behind my back. But no one ever mentioned a thing, and I never noticed.

I want to feel ticked off, but most of all I just feel sad, like, left out.

I look up from the paperwork just in time to see the intersection of Radar Run Road and Fillmore Avenue approaching much too fast. "Hang a left," I say, starting to reach for the wheel. But I'm too late. The Beetle rockets by the parking lot of Viking Ice Cream and sideswipes a stop sign before Gus comes to his senses and jerks us into a thirty-mile-an-hour U-turn. We spin out, laying a streak of rubber across the dotted yellow line and up onto the curb. The world wobbles to a standstill and my neck pulls against the rest of me like a rubber band about to snap.

As the Beetle shudders, I catch my breath, the world whirling outside the open windows.

I stick my face out to take in some air, and then notice the thunderclouds that have ganged up around the taller buildings of downtown Southworth and washed over the horizon. Then I hear it: a soft rattle as the raindrops spit down onto the warm and empty streets.

In this spooky calm, Gus eases up on the brake and, muffler sputtering and headlights off, eases us into the parking lot of Viking Ice Cream.

Viking's insides glow with clear golden light. Everything is visible through the big front window, where Kurt's direct hit with a fake ice cream fastball has left the glass busted into jagged lines.

A family eats in a booth on one side of the parlor, the three squirming kids barking and unable to sit still. On the other side, a lonely high school student slouches over the long blue counter gobbling a Please Clean Up After Your Dog—all by himself on a Sunday night, the night before the last week of school. Behind the counter a duo of overweight cooks in novelty Viking helmets glare at the clock on the wall, watching every minute pass as they take turns scraping the grease off a skillet with a crusty blade.

Listening to the soft hum of rain on the car roof and its soothing tap on the concrete, I'd like to believe that this whole night might end peacefully. That even with all that's happened, a treaty can be arranged, a cease-fire.

Then Gus, who I thought had dozed off, leans over and says in my ear, "What's he drive?"

I think about the question, and then touch my fingertip to the wet windshield in front of me. "That," I say.

Back by the Dumpster and partially hidden by a ring of plump black and green trash bags, Kurt appears, pushing his Yamaha across the asphalt. A french fry sticks out from the corner of his mouth like a toothpick. He disappears behind Viking again, then returns, his arms piled high with steaming sacks of takeout.

"Dude's stocking up," Gus says.

"I can't believe he came back here," I say. Does Kurt not know any better? Coming back to Viking is such a brainless move that I almost feel sorry for the big oaf.

As grease eats away at the paper sacks in his arms, Kurt steadies a beverage carrier on the moped handlebars and tries to start the engine. But the keys drop from his overloaded hands into a growing puddle on the blacktop.

Things are about to get worse. The manager of Viking Ice Cream throws open the side door of the restaurant and shouts something garbled. My brother ignores him the same way he tunes out everything and everyone else, the same way he ignored this loser during their first go-round. But this time the guy yanks a cell phone off his belt, flips it open, and waves it around like he's holding a live grenade. Still, my lovable brother keeps his ass pointed squarely in the guy's flustered face.

"Dude never should have stopped for burgers," Gus says. I nod in agreement, my sweaty hand stuck to the door handle.

Viking's manager keeps trying to get Kurt's attention, but eventually, much to my relief, gives up and throws his arms above his head in frustration. As he turns to leave, the guy twitches, and it looks like he might just reach over and shove the Yamaha over. Instead, he closes his eyes and mouths something, and then turns and rushes back inside, slamming the door so hard that I can hear it from here.

This is when I should get out and walk over to my brother. Kurt's back is to me now, as he tries to fit all the food into the open storage compartment. I could just stroll up and tap him on the shoulder.

Then I hear the police sirens. They cut through the deafening stomp of the thunderstorm.

That's it. My moment to get out and walk over is way gone.

Kurt stiffens, like a dog does when it hears one of those high-pitched training whistles. He shoves the sacks into the storage compartment, crushing them, and slams the lid. Then he leaps onto the Yamaha from behind, no hands. As the police sirens approach, only blocks away now, dry heads start to poke from the windows of parked cars. Through the falling rain, I can make out the manager of Viking standing up close to the front window, grinning like a psycho through that spiderweb of shattered glass.

I look back toward the Dumpster, but Kurt's gone, already a block away, his back wheel cutting a fan of water up from the gutter. The downpour falls all around and shimmers like tinsel in our dim headlights.

"Go!" I tell Gus. "Follow him."

We race out of the parking lot and then barrel south down Millard Fillmore Avenue like a cannonball, back in the direction from which we came. Kurt shrinks to a dot in the blotchy darkness and slips between and around lit shapes that could be cars or could be houses—it's too hard to see. The storm blows sheets of water sideways against the Beetle, and gust after gust pounds the windshield, making the dashboard tremble. The music on the radio sounds so broken, it could be just tuneless static.

Kurt is trying desperately to get away, but if I know one thing for sure, it's that Kurt is not used to being chased. This time I am the one chasing him, instead of the other way around. He gets farther away, becoming little more than a streak of light on the road, a trick of the eye. He's there one second and gone the next; no matter what happens, I can't let him get away.

We stay close, zooming by the school again and

turning east into the maze of side streets across from the quarry turnoff. The roads in these neighborhoods have decayed into uneven stretches of pavement, strewn with upended chunks of asphalt. Gus attempts to dodge every obstacle, but we seem to end up bouncing in and out of ruts the size of foxholes.

At one point a huge pool of standing water spans an intersection ahead of us, and Gus sees it too late, leaving us no choice but to surf right on in. The water level rises so high that it threatens to seep in through the door cracks. The Beetle's poor engine gurgles, but coughs and roars on. Gus pumps his fist and howls, as though he has just personally kicked Mother Nature in the ass. Behind us, police sirens whine in the rain, though I have yet to see a single spinning light.

By now Gus has positioned his face an inch or so from the windshield, with the hope of recognizing the giant smear that has become our insignificant suburb. We sail on, guided by the beacon of Kurt's red-square brake light, and turn onto Old Quarry Road going south. Soon I can make out the warehouses of the Snud plant as they rise up sharp against the night like islands in an angry ocean.

That's when Kurt really tries to lose us. He veers off the road and hops the curb with a sweet trick that would be so much cooler if it wasn't for the fact that we are being chased by cops and driving through about two feet of oily ooze. Reliable Gus doesn't hesitate, and jolts us over the curb, which sends me flying up off my seat and against the chest strap of my seat belt. I wince, swearing as the car skims through a stew of drowned weeds and scrapes along a lean-to of corrugated steel, making tiny sparks that fizzle through the sheets of rain.

And just like that, our wild ride is over as the Beetle's tires bog down in slime. Gus hits the gas, churning arcs of brown slop across the hood, but within a few seconds a burned chemical smell drifts from the dash and floor vents, filling the car. After a monumental beating that will go down in Southworth history, Rose Purdy's vintage Volkswagen Beetle quits once and for all, and with a relieved and dreamy gasp, it dies.

The headlights still shine ahead of us, holding Kurt in their weak gray beams. He has problems of his own. With a sound like two cats strangling each other, the moped seizes up in the mud and pitches Kurt headfirst over the handlebars. With a blank look of surprise across his zitty face, mouth in an O so perfectly round that it looks painted on, he lands spread-eagle in a pool of slop.

I ram the entirety of section C down the back of my pants and then grab the door handle. "Come on," I say to Gus as I swing the door open and let in the rain.

Gus does not share my enthusiasm. He halfheartedly returns my gaze with bloodshot and baggy eyes. "I'm slow as hell, dude," he says. "I think this is as far as I go."

"Well, thanks for the lift," I say, and as I step out into the storm, I see Gus fire up a joint and recline his seat all the way back until he disappears. One freckled hand rises up to flash me the peace sign and then turn up that god-awful music on the radio.

Twenty feet in front of me, Kurt stomps on his moped's starter, but it doesn't want to catch. Like a nutcase, he kicks the pedal again and again, until it actually breaks off, and as the pedal falls, the Yamaha comes to life. It buzzes like a chain saw and shoots a trail of smoke from the exhaust pipe.

But I can't let him leave. So, as screaming gales hurl hard bits of water against my cheeks like nails kept in a refrigerator, I trudge toward him. My heart seems to sink to the pit of my stomach, then shoot to the top of my throat. Up and down, like one of those hammer-and-bell games at the carnival. I lose both shoes to the deepening sludge, but I break into a run, moving faster and faster toward him until I reach ramming speed.

Just as Kurt lifts the bike from its sinkhole, I connect with his massive mutant chest. It's like running headfirst into a brick wall.

"Blurg," he grunts as we tumble over and do a double face-plant in the mud. We land awkwardly, and our noses crack against each other, which makes both of us yell a word that, five years ago, would have definitely gotten our mouths washed out with soap. My head rings, and when I crawl to my feet, Kurt has fled again, the abandoned Yamaha sputtering in the muck. Its storage compartment hangs open, trickling chili dogs and textbooks.

Through the rain I catch movement beside a collapsed garage—a white shirt hovering through sheets of fuzzy rain. Thunder cracks, and I take off after him, six steps for every two of his. Pain flashes through my injured foot every time it nails the ground, but I keep going. I dodge dented hubcaps and jump rotten railroad ties, scurry over downed chain-link and into a sunken ditch, weave around a pyramid of oil drums to the main Snud warehouse, with its busted window wells. I slow down to look for signs of life, but no one is home.

I hear splashing steps from inside the warehouse and then, as if by pure instinct, flop onto my stomach and worm my way past the snapped-off and filed-down bars of the window well. Losing control I start to slide and then spin head over heels through the air into a puddle that would be better described as a miniature lake.

I come to the surface in a daze. A milky brown substance that's half water, half mud pours from the broken basement windows and spreads across the warehouse floor like lava. Most of it collects in my corner, where the floor seems lower than everywhere else. Blobs of glass and aluminum bob along in the slow spiraling current. Curtains of falling water stream through gashes in the roof and arc down in small waterfalls that break on the catwalks and scattered machines.

Kurt shuffles weakly through a shallow area on the other side of the room, and then out a delivery-entrance door that hangs ajar.

This place is finished, a tomb littered with random reminders of the kids that came before me. Wicked Witch's old black-and-white TV lies on the iron catwalk above, knocked from its windowsill. The cord hangs over the railing as drops of water slide along the rubber and make it drip like a crazy IV. Passing the office that Kerouac used for my Affront initiation, I stick my head inside, only to find that the place has been completely wiped down. Nothing remains from that night, not a file folder or binder, not a plastic wrapper or its matching red pin. The only evidence that people had even set foot in this place after 1970 is a washed-out baby photo tacked to a bulletin board on the wall, and of course, the naughty graffiti hacked into the desktop.

I should have known that none of this was ever out of Kerouac's control, and he had probably plotted it all carefully from day one. Even now, as I finally come around to what needs to be done. The bastard didn't miss a thing. I might even laugh if my mouth wasn't full of mud.

The rain slows as I near the open delivery door, and when I exit the Snud warehouse, I can see the swollen clouds shoving off. Above me the old water tower glows in a sliver of moonlight, filling the sky with that weird motto—SNUD KNOWS FIZZ—like a message beamed down from God. There are no police on our tail, and no Affront, and no principal—it's only Kurt and me now.

He stumbles forward through the easing sprinkle, trying to stay on his feet long enough to make it to the small crooked guard shack that sits beside the security gate. He leans forward, like he's very slowly falling over.

When he reaches the shack, Kurt fumbles with the lock and unlatches it, and then throws the door open. I'm too tired to wonder how he knows the combination. Maybe Kerouac gave it to him.

Covering the last few yards to the shack, I look up and see that crooked row of makeshift factory homes sitting as they've sat for half a century, lording over the gloomy landscape. They look so small, as if I could reach up and flick them over like a line of dominoes.

I take the few last steps, over two orange extension cords, and end up standing in the doorway of the shack, resting against the doorframe. The thick extension cords lead along the ground to the power pole beside the warehouse. The small shack links right into Affront's network, as though tied to the end of a winding leash.

So this is where he always goes to hide. I might be the only other human being ever to set foot into my brother's little lair.

I would call it a roomy outhouse, if not for its lack of a toilet and the appropriate stench. A section of blue scrap carpet has been thrown down to keep the floor from just being dirt, and a handyman's hook lamp hangs from a nail on the roof on an orange extension cord. Kurt's plugged it in. The lamp gives off a grainy haze that is not really dark and not really light, but more like what you see when you're so exhausted you could sleep standing up.

Maps from *National Geographic* magazines sag from the walls, and alone in the shack's corner flops a beanbag chair that I recognize from our basement, a stinky old thing that made the whole downstairs smell like cheese. In the other corner stands a tall knobby-legged desk meant for one person, like some kind of antique. Several short stacks of books sit on the scrap of carpet, divided into subjects like *Literature, French,* and *Metallurgy.* As I pant in the doorway, water drips from the ceiling all over the books, where previous water stains have warped and discolored the covers.

"Kurt," I say. That's all.

He sits at the desk and cries, and his tears drop on the red-ink scribbles that deface the countless worksheets and term papers and quizzes and test prep books that cover the desk.

I walk in and flop onto the smelly old beanbag. So this is Kurt's fun-time playhouse, a crooked closet in a field of junk. It's almost funny. A bulletin board hangs beside the narrow doorway, tilted to one side with the slouch of the shack. Pinned to the corkboard, a Mount Kennedy Military School trifold brochure hangs open. Those uniformed students with their medals and smiles look like they're from some other planet, a better planet than this one.

Then the shack isn't so funny anymore. I imagine Kurt out here alone, reading under the hook lamp. No one in our house has ever gotten a medal for anything.

"Look at me, Kurt," I say, and I sound a lot like Mom when I say it.

But he can't. I take a long, hard look at my twin brother and see him in a dark room walled with books, and it is not at all what I would have imagined.

Across the header of the topmost paper are the words *Below Average, Needs Improvement,* written in skinny red marker.

"I'm screwed, man," Kurt says. His nose is all plugged up, and he sounds like a cartoon character. "I didn't do anything to Millie." His huge swollen eyes turn to me in my beanbag. "I swear I didn't."

Now I'm the one who wants to run away. Damn these short legs.

"About Millie . . ." I say.

VOICES FROM THE VOID

At long last the rain clears and leaves the world muddy brown. The moon sticks its head out from under a fuzzy hat of cloud that seems to be chugging off north, for Cleveland, maybe.

I give Kurt the soda first and then hand up the How I Learned to Love the Bomb, which he snatches hungrily, eyeing all five whipped-creamy bananas as if deciding which one to devour first is a life-or-death decision. He puts the cardboard tray aside and then crawls to the edge of the huge telescope dish to give me his hand. I cling to the base about fifteen feet from the ground, like a cat stuck up a tree.

Hanging down from the edge, Kurt stretches out and pulls me up as if I weigh less than nothing.

It is almost two in the morning according to the clock in Viking Ice Cream, the ticking hands of which are a bloody Viking spear and a hunter's horn. They must often get oddballs in there at two in the morning, because when I showed up at the counter in clothes so soaked brown I could have lain outside in the grass and gone camouflage, the two apron-wearing Vikings hardly blinked.

After fetching the sundae, I followed Kurt through the field outside and then over the fence into the over-grown land of the radio telescope observatory. Then we bushwhacked our way through high grass and weeds below the giant metal dishes to a clump of trees, where Kurt had a backpack tied up in some branches near the ground. He must hang out here all the time, because inside a plastic bag I found bottles of pop, water, a radio, a flashlight, and a picture of Grampa in his old BORN TO SHOP T-shirt.

The ground is far below me now as I find my bal-ance in the gigantic sloping dish. The telescope must be about thirty or forty feet in diameter and has a big pointy thing jutting out of the center toward the moon. The bottom is made of many individual panels with gaps here and there, and I have to step carefully, so as not to sprain my ankle, and lightly, so as not to alert the college astronomy department that there is an impending alien invasion.

A few of the panels on the lower end of the dish have giant dents, and they've gathered about six inches of clear rainwater. It's the best seat in the house, so Kurt and I scoop with our cupped hands, like we're bailing out a sinking ship, but soon enough we get tired and sit our cabooses right down in that standing water. Together we stare out over the twinkle of Viking Ice Cream, and the blinking broadcast towers of the community college, chilling like we're a couple of guys sitting in a baby pool on a regular summer day.

Kurt hasn't said much since I caught him in his little shack.

All he said was, "You want to get out of here?" which we did, because after everything that had happened, all I wanted was to get the hell "out of here."

This big kid gobbling ice cream next to me is a question mark, and I stare right at him as he eats, like he has some physical deformity that I can't take my eyes off of. We see each other every day, all the while existing in two very separate universes that surround us like protective space suits. After so long in those bubbles, it's no wonder we forgot what life was like on the outside, what it's like when those little universes don't pass by each other but collide.

"What are you looking at?" he says, mouth mushy with banana.

"You," I say. He looks a lot like me, only older, even older than he should look. He has stubble, and a tattoo on his lower belly that I've never seen before, some kind of Chinese character that presses up against the dirty white T-shirt plastered to his skin.

The crickets have stopped for once, and the fields spread out around us dark green and trickling. Two cars have arrived since we got here, and they sit parked under the treetops, idling.

"Stop looking at me," Kurt says. "You're freaking me out."

"Sorry," I say. Why did he bring me here?

Kurt licks his spoon a few times to make sure he's gotten every last fleck of chocolate syrup and then tosses it over the edge of the dish. "You know, I saw Dad," he says. And he says it just as he tips back the empty cardboard tray to guzzle down the pooled banana goop.

My throat closes. "You saw him?"

I consider the information, looking up at the stars overhead. In my memory I can still make out the assortment of mug shots glaring up at me from the red Affront binder. Dad, who is a total stranger to me, squints at the camera in every shot, as though he plans to pull a gun and mug the photographer.

"He came over," Kurt says. "He called me up that day you walked in on me. He said he wanted to talk, be like buddies or something."

My father left us when he found out that I might have a medical condition, a problem, one he didn't want to deal with. There were other reasons, too, but that was the straw that broke the family's back. I guess he couldn't handle it. Too much reality for a simple guy who had spent most of his adult life passed out in a strip club called Juggernauts.

Problem is, I don't know who got hurt worse. Me, for being Dad's reason for leaving, or Kurt, for not being an important enough reason for Dad to stay.

Kurt sighs, and right then the whole radar dish shifts, moving several inches to the left. It makes the water slosh and sprinkle down through the gaps in the panels.

We scramble for the nearest handholds, but the dish stops moving and settles with a steady hum.

Once I'm settled, too, I say, "So are you and Dad, like, friends now?" I'm not sure if I should feel jealous, or really, really lucky that Kurt was the one who saw Dad, and not me.

"No," Kurt says. "All he wanted was money. He wanted me to get it from Mom."

"Steal it?" I say.

"Yeah," Kurt says, and shakes his head violently. "I hadn't seen him in, like, two years, and he looked like crap. I didn't know what to do. You know, I always worried that there was no way for me to avoid becoming just like him. I actually felt myself getting that way—dirty, mean, and stupid. Kind of like you always thought I was." He shoots me a pissed-off look and then continues. "After seeing him that time, I knew I had to do something. No more screwing around, no more drugs, no more skipping school."

"Why didn't you tell someone?" I say. Down in the field, a car horn honks, a couple accidentally stepping on the wheel while in the throes of meaningless ecstasy.

"I did," Kurt says. "I told Mom and then I talked to Ms. Wessin."

"What about me?" I say. I'm sure I would have understood. Hell, it would have changed everything. We could have been friends, gotten along like the Wonder Twins or something.

Instead of answering, Kurt smirks at me. "Just like you say, I'm not the smartest guy around," he says. "Not like you. I guess I thought you'd make fun of me like you always do."

"What does that mean?" I say.

The base of the telescope rumbles and then the dish convulses, jarring us off our butts. I slide a few feet toward the lip of the dish and then stop, adjusting as the mechanical whir shuts down again.

"Tell me what that means," I say. "Make fun of you like I 'always do'?"

"I don't know," Kurt says, turning around in his seat so his entire mammoth body faces me, due south across town.

"*You're* the asshole," I say.

"Why, because I'm big?" he says. "You think I like being this way?" He grits his giant, nasty ice-cube teeth like I've seen him do a million times, before punching a hole in the drywall or breaking off the legs of a kitchen chair by beating it against the counter.

"Being what way?" That's it. I've listened to enough of Kurt's crap.

"Being me," he says. "A big ape. This." He gestures up and down his body, like a spokesmodel showing off the features of a brand-new flat-screen TV. "I hate it," he says.

"Being big sucks, huh?" I say, splashing a handful of water into his face. "At least your feet don't dangle when you sit on the can."

His face shrivels up as if he's just had the air knocked out of him. "You're so mean, Arty," he says, shaking his head.

"*I'm* mean?" I say. Where has this guy been, living in another dimension, where tall people are short and fat people skinny, where pretty girls are really as nice as they look?

"Hell yes," he says. "When I got that letter from Mary, it killed me, man. It gutted me. And *you* wrote them. Yeah, you're mean. Every word out of your big mouth is mean." He slams his kneecap with a big boulder of a fist. "I don't know if it's the hormone thing or the drugs, but ever since you stayed small, you've been all over me. You know, it wasn't easy for me, either, when Dad took off and Mom was totally obsessed with you. It was like I fell off the freaking planet."

"That was almost two years ago," I say. "Get over it."

"*You* get over it!" he snaps and shoves me hard up against the side of the dish.

I push him back, slipping all over the place with my wet sneakers. "You stuffed me in the chest, Kurt," I say. I don't need to tell him that, but I want to, anyway, because I never have before. In case he forgot. In case he didn't think it was a big deal that he locked me in a chest overnight. It was like being buried alive.

"I know," he says. He clenches his hair in his hands and pulls. "I'm sorry, I'm sorry."

"You should be sorry," I say. "You should be sorry until you're dead, you big freak."

"Do you remember that day?" he says. A fartlike sniffle escapes his bloated nose.

"I remember."

"Do you remember why I put you in there?" he says.

I must have blocked it out, because my head gets stuck in the darkness of it, what it felt like to pound on that thick, dusty wooden lid, the sound of the lock as it rattled.

"You wouldn't stop," Kurt says. "You called me *stupid* and *gorilla* and *idiot* and *ogre*. You wouldn't leave me alone, Arty. I just wanted you to shut up and go away."

"You didn't have to lock me up," I say. "I'm smaller than you."

Then, as if he's still growing, Kurt stands up and bears down on me with all that stored rage. "That's not my fault!" he shouts.

I open my mouth to let him have it. I want to punch him right in the zits, to kill him with every last angry word I can find.

But I can't find any, because he's right.

Kurt stares at me. His cheeks are flushed and puffs of spittle stick to his lips.

"I know," I say. "I'm sorry."

His face becomes blank, confused. He eases back down on his haunches.

"Okay," he says.

What would our dud of a dad say if he could see his two equally idiotic sons basting like a couple of turkeys in this muddy rainwater, our butt cheeks probably wrinkling like fingertips in the bathtub? It's a good thing we'll never have to know.

And Grampa? He'd crack the hell up.

It's just the three of us now—Mom and Kurt and me—and I guess that's how we'll have to play it.

Taking a deep breath, I slide over and pull the black flashlight from Kurt's plastic bag and then click the button. A tunnel of clean light bolts up into space.

"What are you doing?" Kurt says.

"We've had a lot of luck around here lately," I say, flattening out on my stomach and wriggling toward the edge of the sloping dish. "We even had a grand slam a week ago."

Kurt's eyes widen, and he drops down on all fours and crawls down next to me. "A grand slam? We never, ever saw a grand slam."

"I know," I say. "Which is why it was so very exciting." Giving him the flashlight, I fold my arms out in front of me and rest my chin on my knuckles. The weight of the knob-pendant presses cool against my throat.

"Looks pretty quiet down there," he says, swinging the flashlight beam through the trees.

"You're going to military school, huh?" I say. So this is what it means to always see the good things, not because you have to but because you *want* to. Even if no one else sees them.

He looks up at me and the traces of a smile pass over his face. "I don't know yet," he says. "The entrance tests are in July."

"You wanna be a Navy SEAL or something?" I say.

"No," he says. "I just want a change, you know?"

"Yeah," I say. "I know."

For once I don't need to think about what to do next. With a small tug, I bring the drawer knob out from under my shirt and pull the necklace over my head.

"Here," and I give it to him.

"Hey, that's mine," he says, taking it. He looks at it and then looks at me, but neither one of us says anything. Putting on the necklace, he pulls himself up into a sitting position on the lip of the dish. His long legs hang over the edge, and he swings them back and forth like a little kid. I smile because as much as I liked wearing that knob, I feel better with the weird weight gone.

"Third base!" Kurt says suddenly, pointing. He directs the flashlight's glow down like an expert. "In the white one, there's a girl with her top off."

I strain my eyes but can't make out any details in all that darkness.

"Hey!" Kurt yells through a cupped hand. "Hey, down there!"

"Who is that?" a boy yells back from the front seat of the car.

"Move to your left!" Kurt shouts.

"What?"

I sigh. If you want something done right, you have to do it yourself. "Could you stay in the light, please?" I call down. "We're trying really hard to see your girl-friend naked!"

Kurt stifles a laugh and jabs my shoulder blade. Then, suddenly remembering, he bites his lip and looks over at me. "What are we going to do about Millie?" he says.

He's right. Once we leave this dish, we'll have to face the music. Mom's going to be so pissed. "Don't worry, we'll think of something," I say. "*I'll* think of something."

The overgrown fields lie silent for a minute, before the lone white Jetta starts up and Leslie Dermott and Vincent Nguyen drive off across the gravel for home.

APPOMATTOX SCHOOLHOUSE

M s. Wessin stops guzzling her root beer and sniffs. She has one of those colds that's going around. She starts talking again, anyway, even though it must kill her throat, and between sentences she chews her fingernails down to nubbins. Any other Monday night, she'd probably be having a one-woman romantic comedy marathon, taking breaks between beers to check her progress in some online singles chat room. Or maybe I'm just being mean. Apparently I have a tendency to do that.

The four of us—Wessin, Mom, Kurt, and me—sit around a plastic patio table in the Fillmore High teachers' lounge, sipping free drinks from the vending machine. It's a testament to the value that Southworth places on its schoolteachers to see that every choice on the machine is a genuine Snud product, an outdated roster of Depression-era soda pop. I still can't figure out where people get this stuff.

We are discussing the future here today, because it actually looks like we might have one. The Moores of Southworth, Ohio, are not finished yet, not if the police department, Principal Malone, Mount Kennedy Military School, and a herd of red-pinned miscreants have anything to say about it. We are this community's greatest project, so much so that we should get our own grant.

We sit and let Ms. Wessin's words sink in. She has told my mother everything as the police have told to her, and now we sit and wait. Of course, we Moores excel at sitting around tables silently staring at one another. We are the champions of the uncomfortable silence. Some people call those family meetings—ours are more like séances.

After Grampa died we convened around the kids' LEGO play table in the hospital waiting room, teary, our sleep-deprived faces stretched into sad shapes. Mom's cheeks had deflated so much that she looked like a popped gum bubble.

Then, when I was diagnosed with Growth Hormone Deficiency, we accidentally got into an argument around the condiments stand at the Wendy's salad bar. I said I didn't want therapy, and Mom said I didn't have a choice. As Mom lectured me, Kurt listened and licked ranch dressing off the serving spoon that everyone in the place was expected to use. I remember how when we left the restaurant, Mom turned the car stereo up superloud so we couldn't hear her taking weepy gulps of air in the front seat. Even with Rod Stewart mooing through the wimpy speakers, we still knew she was crying.

Wessin breaks the silence and directs her teacher's gaze at Mom. "Does that all make sense, Ms. Moore? Do you want me to go over it again?"

Mom shakes her head. She sits in a state of shock, rolling a cigarette back and forth across the tabletop.

"We're here tonight to discuss how best for Kurt to confess," Ms. Wessin says. "So far he has been unwilling to cooperate with the authorities, but I have volunteered to step in and help."

"What if I have nothing to confess?" Kurt says. He's scared. It's obvious in the way his voice has gone up a whole octave.

"That means we still have something to talk about," Ms. Wessin says. "Go ahead, Kurt."

This is when Kurt surprises me. Whereas I have the puppy-dog eyes mastered from years of being locked in a child's body, he has turned the dumb-as-a-post stare into an art form. For a second I can't tell if he even notices Ms. Wessin's presence, much less understands the words firing from her mouth.

"Nothing," he says at last. It is not a word but a noise, a single smudged letter that could be consonant or vowel but sounds like no noise I've ever heard. "I don't know anything."

With that, Kurt proves me wrong about everything I've ever said about him. He's smart enough to act stupid when it gets him what he wants. And right now, he wants Wessin to turn her spotlight elsewhere, which is exactly what she does. Mission accomplished.

The open windows bring in fresh air from outside. It shakes the leaves of the plastic plants on the sill, and sends the smell of newly cut grass blowing across the table. Outside, the roar of the lawn mower rises and falls over the afternoon quiet. By the door a photo calendar of wiener dogs in dresses hangs from a nail on the wall. A star of orange highlighter surrounds the last day of school—June 11—and above it the words: YOU'RE GODDAMN RIGHT.

"What about you, Arty?" Ms. Wessin says. "Do you have anything to offer?" Three heads rotate slowly my way.

I have a generic store brand bandage with advanced skin-tone Fiberwear technology plastered across my nose. So does Kurt. We look like mirror images again, if only a tiny bit, like two guys recuperating from nose jobs by the same nearsighted doctor.

I wonder if I can do this. I've always been the good guy.

"Arty," Mom says, "you heard Ms. Wessin. Tell us what you know."

"Kurt can't confess, because he didn't steal Millie," I say. "I did."

"What?" Mom says.

The room goes silent. The wiener dogs on the calendar are the only ones not gawking at me. They gaze at a butterfly that sits on a daisy in the corner of the photograph.

"Are you serious, Arty?" Ms. Wessin says.

"How's this for serious?" I say, and bring out Millie's big chunky eyeball, my killer's trophy. It makes a thud as it hits the tabletop, and Mom jolts when she sees it, like she's just seen her first corpse.

Kurt utters a gravelly "Whoa" under his breath.

I look right at Mom. "I told you he didn't do it," I say.

"Just because you have a piece of the statue doesn't mean anything," Ms. Wessin says quickly. She senses I'm up to something. First, she will pretend not to care and roll her eyes like she's too cool to play my little game. But then, she'll try to be my friend again, because people like her hate being the bad cop. They'll do anything for a person's love, even a tiny little nobody like me. That's how I know I will win.

"You want to hear how I did it?" I say.

"This is going to be sweet," Kurt mutters.

"Don't encourage him," Mom hisses.

Ms. Wessin tries to stop me. "Arty, don't you—"

"First," I say, "I had to drug all the neighborhood dogs with hot dogs laced with cold medicine. That was the easy part. Then, I broke into the school maintenance shed and took the old tractor they use to mow the football field."

"Let me guess, you pulled over the statue?" Ms. Wessin says, frowning.

"I tugged that sucker down like I was pulling over a statue of Stalin," I say. "I was liberating Millard Fillmore High School, and it didn't even know it needed me to."

There is no humor in Ms. Wessin's voice, and Mom and Kurt are too dumbfounded to speak. "And I suppose you drove right down the middle of the street on a lawn mower dragging a giant turtle? Am I close?" she says.

"Not the whole time," I say. "I had to stop to siphon gas from a parked car. I used a straw. It's not as easy as you'd think."

"You expect me to believe this?" Ms. Wessin says.

"If it's the truth," I say.

"Is it the truth?" she says.

"Sure."

Crossing her arms, Ms. Wessin watches me closely. She's beginning to crack already. I can almost see the hairline fractures.

"I'm not done," I say. "When I got Millie away from school, I had to get rid of her fast. So I took her to the all-night copy place and shipped her to myself, two-day delivery."

"You should have told me," Ms. Wessin says. "You could have used the school's FedEx account."

"Well, I've got the tracking number," I say. "Maybe we can get a refund." I do not have the number, because, of course, there is none.

"Stop it, Arty; this is a waste of time," Mom says. "You've got nothing to prove."

"Stop what?" I say.

"We get the joke," Ms. Wessin says. "There's no need to keep going."

"What joke?" I say, gathering momentum. "I did it. It was all me."

"Damn it, Arty," Mom says. She clasps her hands in front of her, and I half expect her to start praying. The unlit cigarette in her fingers is cracked, dangling by a shred of paper. She is trying to bend my will like some psychics bend spoons.

"So tell me," Ms. Wessin says, "how in the world did you get that thousand-pound statue up above the quarry?"

"Elementary, my dear Wessin," I say. "I constructed a complex system of pulleys using a number of Expando-Flex workout machines from the school gym."

"You mean Iron Abs?" Kurt says.

"Yes, that's right," I say, smiling politely at Kurt. "Iron Abs."

"Wow," Ms. Wessin says. "It's good someone found a use for those things. They certainly don't do what they advertise." She smiles. It's odd. Wessin is up to something, too. I can tell.

Mom sinks lower into her chair and stops listening. She has checked out, given up. When it comes to being associated with felons—Dad, Kurt, and me—her record is a lousy 0–3.

"What happened next?" Kurt says.

Suddenly Mom comes back to life. "You!" She points across the table at Kurt, her blue fingernail glinting in the fluorescent lights. "You be quiet." Then she slides back down until she's just a lump.

"Well," I say, coming to my grand finale, "then I hung Millie's sorry turtle ass off that cliff. And after that, she fell. I only wish she could have taken out a couple of those police cars on her way down."

"That would have been awesome," Kurt says. And I know he's picturing all sorts of explosions and mayhem in that thick head of his.

This is actually kind of fun, like writing those fake love letters. Even though Mom and Ms. Wessin have been left in the dust and are now just suffering through every word, Kurt seems to like my story. It feels good.

"That's pretty unbelievable," Ms. Wessin says. She's right. But I know that the police have nothing tying Kurt to Millie but a single anonymous note and a bunch of random rubble. Me, I've got a turtle's eyeball and a story—and it's a story they want.

Who knows? Maybe Kurt will go on to be a general or an admiral or something at Mount Kennedy Military School. And maybe it's my turn to raise a little hell.

Then, tapping her ballpoint pen on her chin, Ms. Wessin smiles. It's not a hollow-headed smile, either, but the grin of someone remembering a punch line in private. She flashes me her I'm-disappointed-in-this-C+-grade-because-you're-definitely-capable-of-a-B–look. For some reason, I can't look back.

"All right then," she says, nodding. "I'll buy that."

"What?" I say. I can't believe it.

Neither can Mom. "You can't be serious," she says.

"I trust that Arty knows what he's doing," Ms. Wesson says, still grinning like a wacko.

"You wanted a confession," I say. "And that's what I gave you."

"Okay," Ms. Wessin says, "you confessed. Fine." She narrows her eyes, and that's when I catch a glimpse of what she's up to—she's daring me. She's testing to see how far I'll wade out into the dangerous waters before turning and running willy-nilly back to safety.

"Telling a story is easy," she says. "Care to put it in writing?"

"You bet," I say. I have to admit, she's got me sweating.

"We'll see," Ms. Wessin says, but at the same time I see her hand going for the briefcase under the table. I lock eyes with her, something that I usually avoid. Never look a teacher in the eye—it's a fundamental rule, like never run from a bear or never whack a beehive with a stick.

Ms. Wessin knows my brother and me, so she must know what's happening to our family. I have to get her on my side, make her understand why I'm doing this. "I did it," I say. "The whole thing is my fault. I swear."

"I said we'll see," Ms. Wessin says. "Now let's do this." The leather briefcase appears, and from inside it she draws out a sheet of crisp, clean white paper. She is about to place the paper in front of me when she hesitates. As the three of us sit and wait, Ms. Wessin digs deeper into her files and comes out with another sheet of paper much like the first.

"I have to admit," she says, "it all seems pretty ambitious for just one kid." She places the two papers side by side on the table. "There have been rumors flying all over school about a particular group of students, maybe you've heard of them. It just occurred to me that if you did all of this, as you say you did, then you might have had some help. That's not a crazy thing to wonder, is it?"

"No!" Mom almost shouts. "The crazy thing is that you're letting him feed you this bull."

But even Mom can't sway Ms. Wessin from her strategy. That's when I realize that I might have underestimated my frightfully boring, socially awkward, and depressingly homely American studies instructor. It seems there's more to her than bangs and a bargain wardrobe after all. And I like it.

"Well?" Ms. Wessin says, licking the tip of her ballpoint pen.

"Sorry," I say, and shrug. "Like I said, I worked alone. I must just have short guys' syndrome, like Napoléon did."

She turns to Kurt, who has no way in hell of pulling off the puppy-dog eyes. In fact, he looks like the kind of guy who would probably placekick a puppy through a goalpost. "What about you, Kurt?" she says. "Do you know of anyone who may have helped your brother?"

It's the "your brother" that gets him, because I really don't know if he thinks of me that way. I haven't given him much reason to.

"Nope," he says.

Ms. Wessin looks back and forth at Kurt and me.

Then she sighs all deep, and points at the two sheets of paper on the table.

On the first sheet, I read the typed words: *I, _____, confess to planning and executing the theft of Millard Fillmore High School property with the intent to vandalize, demoralize, and terrorize.* It goes on, but none of the rest could ever be as sweet as that first bit. Reading it gives me a guilty thrill—I've never demoralized or terrorized anyone before. There is a space at the bottom for my signature, and it seems much larger than it needs to be for one name.

The second sheet is blank, but I understand why it's there.

Wessin taps the first paper with her ballpoint pen and then makes eye contact again. "You can sign the confession," she says. "But if you sign it, then that means you're taking all of this on by yourself. Just you." Her eyes seem to focus harder on me when she says the last part.

She places the second sheet over top of the first one, so that the latter disappears. "Or, you can give us names," she says. "One, five, fifty—I don't care." She holds out the pen.

I take it and then look back at her without missing a beat. She trusts me, just like she said she wanted to. But I still have to play the part, and so I bat my child-sized eyelashes and fire up the innocent look all kids use when they ask stupid questions like: *Are boys and girls really different?* It works, every time, because adults are always willing to give us young people the benefit of the doubt.

I sign my form-letter confession, just like a good little boy. Then I watch Ms. Wessin slide it into her briefcase—signed, sealed, and waiting to be delivered. Snapping the second sheet off the table, she crumples it into a ball and sends it sailing into a trash can.

Mom watches the whole thing comatose, one eye peeking between the fingers of her right hand.

"Well, Arty," Ms. Wessin says, "this better be the last blemish we see on your permanent record. Okay?"

"Okay," I say. I owe her, big time.

But what Wessin, and everyone else, doesn't know is that I keep track of my own permanent record, blemishes and all. And that's the record that really matters.

"Let's move on then, shall we?" she says, giving up once and for all on cracking me. It seems Affront and its schizophrenic agenda will remain a secret for now.

I fire a triumphant look over at Kurt and he returns it, his eyes now brighter and his fat face filled with a smile. It feels good to take a bullet for a friend, even if he is my brother.

Outside in the hall the bell rings, and echoes down the long, empty corridors. The janitor pushes the electric floor polisher by the open doorway, whistling. I detect the fresh scent of floor cleaner filling the room. I look at the clock on the wall and wonder what we're going to have for dinner.

Smiling, Kurt shakes his Constellation Root Beer and, when he doesn't hear any splashes, lifts the can and crunches it against his forehead, frat guy style. After that he seems completely at ease. He even smiles a couple of times, that red-jeweled knob dangling from his giant neck.

Afterward in the parking lot, Mom offers to take the two of us for ice cream, but I decline.

"I'm going for a walk," I tell her.

Kurt stands at the open car door and watches me go. Now that he might be going to military school a bunch of states away, I kind of wish he wasn't in such a hurry to leave. I wonder if he feels the same way.

Mom waves as they pull out of the parking lot and onto Ninth-Green Street, headed for home. She drives right by Millie's bleached stone pedestal, where flowers left in mourning have all died and dried up. Then, in the blink of an eye, they're gone, away down Pasture Road toward Grampa's old Victorian, with its saggy roof and overgrown hedges. I'll take my time walking home today, and when I get there, I'll walk right on in and let the screen door bang.

The Fillmore High girls' intramural summer tennis team holds its first practice on the drying green courts alongside the parking lot. The three ball machines they've dragged up next to the net fire volleys, and the girls swat back crazily, like Custer's Last Stand in miniskirts. Tennis balls fall from heaven like comets and make a hollow sound as they hit, zipping off in random directions. The bright sun shines hot in the summer sky.

I see Ms. Wessin propped against a telephone pole watching practice, and her head bobs back and forth as she tracks the balls that ricochet crazily off the girls' rackets.

"Hey, pardner," she says as I approach. "Guess you think you're pretty smart."

"Yeah," I say. "You?"

"Not really," she says, and actually laughs. "I can only imagine the trouble you two guys would get into if you got along." It's a good point, one that reminds me of the old days when I was a kid. Maybe those days are back again. What kind of trouble could we get into now, I wonder?

"What about you, Arty," Wessin says. "Have you ever thought about getting a tutor?"

"No," I say, because I haven't.

"It's been doing your brother a lot of good," she says. "And trust me, kid, you could use a boost in history." She wiggles a scrawny hand in front of her nose as if she smells something bad, like I'm stinking up the place. "On the last test you said that Lewis and Clark commanded the Union and Confederate armies. Do you know how far off that is, kid?"

"According to the test, I think it was about five points off?" I say.

She laughs again, swinging her briefcase. "I think you'll be okay," she says. "But give me a shout if you ever feel like you need boot camp on the Bill of Rights."

"That would be a no," I say.

"Well, call if you need anything," she says.

"Actually, I don't think I have your number."

"Ask your brother."

Then, without any warning, a yellow ball whacks her right in the back of the head.

Feeling

The small leather case waits for me in the mini-fridge. The worn old mitten sits on my desk. The plastic bag spills a dribble of cotton balls across the floor when I pull the chair back. A box of Band-Aids lies open, with the bandages stacked like a deck of cards. Everything is in order.

I feel as if Mom is watching me from the doorway. She taught me how to do this. We practiced on a warm Hot Pocket, pepperoni flavored. We ate it afterward, and we laughed like a couple of maniacs, microwave tomato sauce smeared across our chins.

Cartridges click against each other, syringes roll, and the hormone floats clear and clean in its chamber. I wet a cotton ball and rub the spot where I'm about to get stuck. The smell of the rubbing alcohol fills the musty attic room. I've decided to switch-hit from thigh to thigh to keep either of them from getting jealous.

"You know the drill," Mom used to say. "Think of something good."

I push the plunger in just as the front door bangs shut down on the first floor—all of it happening in one fluid, musical motion.

Think of something . . .

I think of Grampa. I think of sunlit days picking through glinting piles of somebody else's leftovers, somebody else's throwaways. Blue-sky days. Quarry summer days. Days of cleaning up what you mistook for trash but really wasn't. Polishing the beauty that was already there, and then putting it back out into the world.

I wish Grampa were here. I have so many things to ask him. To tell him.

"That's a big boy," Grampa would say. I can almost feel his hand on my shoulder. We walk to the closet together.

The grungy tape measure sings a brand-new song. It drowns out the silence of the closet, the thumping of my heart against my ribs.

Four feet *three* inches tall.

SUPERCONDUCTOR

I match the gaze of the ticket-booth lady and order a ticket for *Superconductor,* a movie the commercials say "will annihilate your senses with an endless assault of mindless stimulation." Mom gave me the money and said I could spend it however I wanted to, as long as I didn't buy a bus ticket to a galaxy far, far away. She said the same thing to Kurt, which is funny, because all he bought was one of those "world's smallest" reading lamps—the nerd.

My first court hearing regarding the great Millie scandal is this Monday, and luckily there's no school to go to afterward. This is my last weekend of true freedom, because who knows what they'll have me doing over the summer, probably just picking up trash on the highway or reading picture books to kids who'd rather be watching TV.

Of course, that's if they can make the confession stick, which they can't. All they have is a signature. None of the stories fit and the evidence is nil. Whoever did trash Millie covered their tracks and then some. I might get off, or I might not. No matter what happens, they'll be messing with the Millie mystery for years, the next great American conspiracy. Except no one outside our little town will ever even hear about it.

Kurt has his entrance exams next month, and until then we're helping Mom clean up the old house a little. We're fertilizing the lawn with some expensive smelly pellets and clipping the hedges back so you can see that there's actually a house underneath. The neighbors must think we just moved in. It's how Grampa would have wanted the old place, a bit more like it was when he lived there a million years ago.

The same troop of geriatrics clunk by me with their walkers, heading for *This Is the First Day of the Rest of Your Death* and leaving rubber-stopper scuffs on the floor. I wonder how many times they've seen that movie.

It doesn't matter, though, because this time I'm seeing what I want to see.

I'm going to sit in the front row and eat a ton of

crap and go deaf from all those sound effects—and love every ridiculous minute of it.

I buy as much junk food as I can carry and weave past the red cords, flipping my ticket to the girl by the podium. I kick open the door to theater six. On the screen a lawyer points out at the audience from a photograph and asks: "Have you been in an accident?" Speakers send out soothing classical music as the picture changes from the lawyer to a cartoon of a cellular phone. "Save my battery and quit yapping," the phone says. I aim for the front center seat and find the whole row empty.

As I get situated, a thrown projectile glances off my neck and falls to the floor. It stings, and when I rub my neck my fingers come up all chocolaty.

"Hey, sit your ass on the seat," a voice says. It is somewhat familiar.

From all the theater silhouettes, I'm able to pick out one tiny form two rows behind me, legs propped up on the seat in front of her. I hear the unmistakable smacks and snapping of a mouth mangling popcorn.

"What do you think you're looking at?" Camilla says. She swings a Twizzler at me like it's a whip and I've been a bad boy. When I don't respond, she flicks her puffiest popcorn kernel right at my face.

"You speak English?" I say.

"*Sí*, big head. Me speaky English," she says. "What

are you doing here, anyway? And where's Dermott—getting her mustache waxed?"

"I think she and me are done," I say.

I see Camilla's blue hair shine in the dim light, trapped under a Cincinnati Reds cap. She wears some punk band's T-shirt and flannel pajama bottoms. Her toes wiggle free in the theater air from the open ends of ripped green high-tops.

"Let's pretend I'm all broken up about this," Camilla says. "That I care. Hey, you had a nice run. Better than most."

"Does she know about you?" I say, not quite knowing what I mean.

"Are you kidding?" Camilla says, and pulls the bill of her baseball cap low over her eyes. "She's as dense as pound cake." Then she motions at me again with her hands, directing, like she's ordering models around a photo shoot. "Could you move? I want to answer movie trivia."

I turn around and lean back in my seat, listening to her suck down a throatful of Raisinets like they're painkillers. It's almost impossible to imagine her in that musty maid costume, or with that vacuum cleaner hose wrapped around her like some crazed python. After seeing her like this, I have trouble picturing her any other way, without those green high-tops and that Reds cap pinching her forehead.

Before I know it I'm tossing a peanut M&M. "Do you want to come up and sit with me?" I say. I wave my arm at the seat stacked with goodies, hoping to somehow lure her in.

"Still don't like the dark, huh?" she says.

"That's not it," I say.

"Maybe next time," she says. "You're a talker. I can't stand talkers."

When I move to sit down again, I feel licorice lash the top of my head. With her dark braid swinging over her shoulder, Camilla stretches over both rows on her tiptoes. I swivel back around only to find her face very close to mine. I smell sugar. "You look different," she says. "Did you do something?"

"I've grown an inch," I say.

"Nice going, Gigantor," she says, and she pats my head like I'm a dog. "Way to go. Now sit."

And as she tears the top off her Milk Duds, I see her red pin reflect in the light of the movie screen. She catches me staring, those perfect green eyes not giving away a thing. She shrugs and sneers, and the music fades up. The previews roll, the theater darkens, and everyone sits back for the show.

I hear her voice. "Yo, King Kong. Down in front."

Down in front.

It's music to my ears.

STATEMENTS THAT ARE ACKNOWLEDGMENT-LiKE iN NATURE

Usually I never say please or thank you for anything. I do what I want and say what I please. (Like that scone you have on your desk—I want it, give it to me.) But this novel has been around the block a few times, and there are people out there to whom I owe a debt of gratitude. Without them this book would either be at the bottom of a file cabinet or being held over my head as blackmail.

First, I'd like to thank my family—John, Jeanie, and the A-Team—for never questioning my urge to make a fool out of myself publicly. Honest, loving support is rare.

Thanks to all of the patient readers and friends who, in one way or another, have endured the voice of Arty Moore through all his incarnations and assorted tantrums: Sharon Darrow, Ron Koertge, Hannah Rodgers, Nell Whiting, and Eileen Zogby.

Additional thanks to those who provided advice and encouragement about this manuscript, even when I probably didn't deserve it: M. T. Anderson, Marion Dane Bauer, and Ellen Levine.

I would also like to express my appreciation to the faculty and staff members of the Vermont College MFA in Writing for Children and Young Adults Program, who have given so many of us open range to graze; also the children, parents, and physicians associated with the Magic Foundation, for their inspiring stories and caring spirit.

Lastly, I would like to thank my literary agent, Barry Goldblatt, who continues to see my future; my amazing editor Michael Stearns, who had faith in my work from before the beginning; and always, my wife, Sarah Zogby, for always being herself—which is always enough.